Eighteen Missing Pages

By Tom Brewster

For information, or to order additional copies, please contact:

Beacon Publishing Group
P.O. Box 41573 Charleston, S.C. 29423
800.817.8480| beaconpublishinggroup.com

Publisher's catalog available by request.

ISBN-13: 978-1-961504-09-7

ISBN-10: 1-961504-09-7

Published in 2024. New York, NY 10001.

First Edition. Printed in the USA.

Eighteen Missing Pages

Chapter One

Abraham Lincoln died April 15, 1865 – murdered by John Wilkes Booth. Before he drew his last breath, his mind loaded with wisdom and brilliance had already been drained into bloody bandages and ceased to exist.

Secretary of War, Edwin Stanton who was a stern and argumentative man was silent as the great man's life slipped away, passing into the deep and unknown depository of souls in the afterlife. Stanton abandoned the harsh and pointed persona he wore like an iron cloak to say softly, "Now he belongs to the ages."

In the aftermath Stanton flew into action in a flurry of moves that would be studied for a century. He called upon a former security agent he had dispatched, under suspicious circumstances, to return to services to track down the assassin and others who were involved. Lafayette Baker, a man who had proven on many occasions that he could not be trusted, was given total reign over the investigation. At breakneck speed Booth and the other offenders were rounded up so quickly that it was as though Baker already knew where they could be found. Booth was lethally shot by Boston Corbertt, a member of a search team headed by Baker's cousin, Luther Baker. Corbertt was borderline insane and so irrational that he cut off his own testicles because he lusted after a woman who was not his wife. In the early stages of the investigation Corbertt himself was suspected of being involved in the assassination.

Booth died of the gunshot wound and the other offenders were jailed or hanged as the wheels of justice trekked along an unfettered track, all greased by Edwin Stanton himself. When all was said and done those fateful words uttered so appropriately by Stanton at the President's deathbed still hold true today. "Now, he belongs to the ages."

Some historical scholars are nervous about Baker and the decision to put him in charge of the most important investigation in American history. Why would a man with such questionable ethics be brought back into service and what were his tactics and sources? Stanton had every investigator and police agent in America at his disposal, but he chose Baker. It's a question still being asked more than a hundred and fifty years later.

Even as Booth lie bleeding to death, evidence was being collected to buttress the action being taken against him. He was alleged to be pointing a gun at Luther Baker when he was shot by Corbertt. His last words were "So another stain on the old banner." No one knows what the statement meant. Might it be that injustice was being committed under cover of the American flag? One of the items confiscated at the scene was Booth's diary. Baker gave the diary to Stanton. It was never used in the proceedings against the eight conspirators who survived to stand trial. It was being held in secret by Stanton until Congress learned of its existence and forced him to relinquish it. Once it was examined it was found to have eighteen missing pages.

Lafayette Baker was astounded when he learned those eighteen pages were gone.

There were numerous strange manifestations that surrounded the events following the assassination, such as Booth's mock burial in the Potomac River. He was actually buried in the dead of night beneath the floor of the old Capitol penitentiary, but not before Stanton made a production of dumping what was supposed to be Booth into the Potomac River.

"*Now he belongs to the ages*," seemed such a profound preponderance that Shakespeare himself could not have uttered so poetically a postmortem salutation to the fallen Commander In Chief. Was Stanton ready for the moment? He was a harsh and hard-spoken man, but in retrospect no other words could have been so tenderly delivered.

A hundred and fifty years later in a small Kentucky town something unbelievable was set in motion, and the man whose fate would be altered was the least likely of participants to be drawn into the fray. His name was Owen Black.

Chapter Two

In 2015, after serving ten years in Navy Special Forces, returning to civilian life was a slow adjustment for Owen Black and the only job he was qualified for was abruptly coming to an end. After 64 years building parts for, General Motors, the plant was being shuttered. Every employee making that long walk through the parking lot was as glum as the condemned headed off to the gallows. Being unemployed at thirty-eight was degrading for Owen, but those guys in the white shirts and ties locking the doors behind them were totally dejected. It was bad enough to be putting the hammer on 400 employees with only eight hours' notice, their last official action was to lock the doors behind them. How easy would it be to find a middle management job when your main interest had been hanging out with your grandchildren?

Owen was sympathetic, but more concerned about his own welfare. His 2010 Ford 150 had only two payments left, Susan's van was paid off, but the house mortgage was hanging in the wind. His girls were enrolled in Meadow Book Baptist School for twenty-five hundred per year each and his savings was nonexistent. Susan taught second grade at Robert E. Lee Elementary School, but public-school teachers in the south were notoriously underpaid. To say things were looking grim was an understatement. Now at 38 he was considering making an appeal to the military to be reinstated.

Owen looked young for his years; physically fit and strong, but the military was particular about allowing first lieutenants back into the ranks without having something special to offer. Owen was a high school graduate, he didn't have technical skills, and his age was a major handicap. His training in service was geared to breaking things and killing people. Now as he was left to contemplate his future, giving Uncle Sam a look even seemed out of reach. Killing people and breaking things had never been palatable to him, but that was when he was twenty years old. Now he fantasized about seeing the world and learning new things. He had never been an outstanding student, but he was smart, curious, and determined. He just wasn't excited about high school. He wanted to walk in the streets of far-away cities, imitate their dialects, eat exotic food, and take in the variegation of world societies. He thought the Navy would provide all of that for him. It just turned out to be something else.

Owen had been a standout in high school sports so basic training was a snap, but Seal training was more hell than he ever wanted to endure again. More times than he could remember he was within feet of ringing the bell signaling that he was dropping out. It wasn't determination stopping him, it was watching the faces of his fellow trainees. The expression in their eyes was indescribable. Some had pity, others stunned curiosity, and yet others exposed the pain of understanding. He knew when that bell rang out there were more than one who would follow him. He didn't want to quit; the watchful eyes of his comrades stiffened his upper lip. He resolved never to quit, and never to quit anything again.

Now as Owen recycled those thoughts with unemployment weighing on his shoulders, his mind was burdened with reality. Killing people and breaking things is necessary, but you have to be a special person to carry that load around with you. He had been in battles when he thought the end was upon him but those slogans that were beaten into his head were never flashing before his eyes as his M-16 rattled endlessly. "Cowards never start – the weak never finish. Give up, give in or give it all you have."

It wasn't his aspiration to put a bullet into a stinking terrorist; it never occurred to him what motivated his enemy to kill, and his own patriotism wasn't ascending skyward in the blue smoke and hot lead exploding from the barrel of his gun pushing him to super heroic feats. He didn't want to die. He wanted to go back to Leesville, Kentucky. He wanted to shoot and take cover. If someone had to die, he wanted it to be the other guy. In the end people died and he was happy it wasn't him. He just didn't fit the description the world held of a Navy Seal. He wasn't fearless. At times he trembled. At times he stayed behind cover until he was safe to advance. Sometimes he was terrified as he advanced into enemy fire, his only thought was to kill that bastard before taking a bullet himself.

In civilian life Owen thought about the things he had done, and it kept him up at night. Even before his discharge when a stranger would shake his hand and thank him for his service, sometimes he wanted to shout, "I was just trying to stay alive!" Owen had not seen the world or experienced the warmth of other cultures. He had killed people and broken things. The thought of going back Into service was abruptly dispersed from his mind. He would rather be standing at an intersection with a cardboard box in front of him stating, "Help me out." Quitting isn't always the worst thing in the world to do. Sometimes not quitting is worse, but he didn't know what was coming for him. His fate was about to change drastically.

Chapter Three

Susan was at the kitchen sink watering a potted plant. Her face was grim and her expression tortured. Owen stopped at the back door, watching her. She was as beautiful at 35 as when they were in high school. Her brown hair was pulled back into a pony-tail, but a few loose hairs were dangling in her eyes. She twisted her mouth to blow the strands aside. All the accolades regarding beauty and grace fit her, but still there was that expression revealing a troubled mind.

She had never wanted to be anything but an elementary school teacher. She would have found better paying work in a bigger city but she loved Leesville; never wanting to be anywhere else. She had been acting withdrawn lately; quiet and introspect. She had stuck with him the entire time he was ''in country,'' worried about his safety, and continually pounded it into his two daughters that he was an all-American hero, but it had not left her unaffected. Something had happened along the way. She had lost that loving feeling. As hard as she tried she wasn't able to rekindle the fire in her heart that attracted her to him. She was hurting inside and angry at herself for losing it.

"We all got pink slips today," Owen said as he walked through the kitchen door.

"Pink slips for what," Susan asked.

"The plant's closing. I'm out of a job"

Susan was quiet. She tightened her upper lip. "How long do you have," she asked.

"No time. They hit us with it this morning. They locked the doors behind us. Most of us wanted to leave as soon as we got the word, but they didn't have our checks ready until four. It sucks!"

Susan dried her hands as she walked to the kitchen table to sit down. Tears were welling in her eyes. Owen followed her to put his hand across her shoulder. She pulled away. She withdrew every time he touched her. Sometimes it was almost imperceptible, but it was always the same. The tears were falling steadily from her eyes. A feeling of dread was building in Owen's chest. He knew his day was spiraling downhill even more than it had already and it didn't have anything to do with being fired.

"This is probably the worst time to tell you this, but I can't do this anymore," Susan said, sitting upright; her voice quivering.

"You can't do what?"

"Our marriage is over, Owen. One of us has to go. I can't do it anymore," she said.

"I can find another job," Owen said. His voice becoming strained. He hated it when his voice was strained. It was a sign of weakness.

"It's not that."

"What is it?" He waited, realizing it was a whole lot more than losing his job. Knowing his emotions were about to take a hit, that question was looming. The question everybody has to ask in that situation, but nobody wants to know the answer. Owen was silently stunned for a moment as the pain and anger began to build in his chest and behind his eyes. "Is there someone else?" he asked quietly. His teeth were clenched in anticipation.

Walking into a firestorm of enemy bullets was easier than what he was going through at that moment. He hoped there would be a lover. It would be easier to take if he had a target for his emotion to find and let loose upon. Someone he didn't know; someone he had no feeling for to unleash a savage assault.

"No, it's just that I don't love you, Owen." She stopped for a long moment. "I mean, I love you, but not the way a woman loves her husband. I don't want to hurt you, and I want you to be happy, but my heart isn't in it."

"We've been together since eighth grade." Owen said, his voice cracking. In all the world this was the one thing that was unthinkable; the one thing he would have bet his life on never happening was happening. He couldn't imagine a life without her in it.

"Living like this isn't fair to either of us. It's especially not fair to you. I spend my days thinking about ways to tell you that we both need to move on. That's not fair. You deserve better."

Owen didn't remember how long he was frozen there, waiting for Susan to change her mind; to tell him that it was a mistake. The afternoon sun faded into the dim light of evening and then to darkness. Lights from cars on the street flashed against the windows, making a dull glow against the walls and shadows inside the room. Susan had gone to their bedroom to cry while he painfully processed her words over and over in his mind. Finally, he walked slowly to the door, onto the porch and then to his truck, still stunned. He was drunk for the next two days.

Chapter Four

The street was damp as a few cars moseyed along in the quiet morning. Owen's pants were damp from sitting on the bench in front of the Navy recruiting office. He was wearing the same clothes for three days; his hair was mussed and grimy; his face covered with a mixture of black and gray stubble. The recruiting officer walked past him, glanced his direction, and then a surprised moment of recognition. "Owen! Is that you?"

Owen was well known in Leesville. He was a decorated war veteran and a former high school sports legend." Everybody is famous in a small town." If you had Owen's background, even more so, but sitting there disheveled and miserable, he didn't look the part.

"Bobby, I need to talk to you," Owen said.

Bobby examined him, still amazed at his appearance. "What the hell happened to you, Owen?"

"It's a long story. I got fired – other stuff too."

"Yeah, I heard they locked you guys out. No notice, nothing. That's some kind of bullshit, man."

"Well, now I need a job. I've wallowed around in self-pity for a few days, but I need to get back to work. I was thinking about re-upping."

"You mean, re-signing for service?" Bobby asked. His expression showing more than just a little doubt.

"Yeah. I know I'd have to take a demotion, but that's okay. I need money and the military benefits. My kids are still in school at Meadow Brook. It costs. My house, too."

"Owen, Owen, Owen… Maaan." Bobby moaned.

Owen was watching Booby's face. He could see the disapproval, as it was intended. His head tilted slightly with an exaggerated grimace on his face. Bobby didn't have to say anything. His body language was saying, "No way are you going back in."

"I know I'm thirty-seven…"

"You're thirty-eight, Owen, nearly thirty nine. You're four years older than me and look where they have me. I'm recruiting in Leesville. I'm too old for most stuff they have out there, and so are you. And besides that------" Bobby hesitated.

"Besides what?" Irritation was mounting in his voice.

"You're damaged, Owen. With all the shit you went through they don't want to take the chance. You know how it is."

Owen was quiet. He pushed his hair back from his forehead. It was thick and dirty standing on end it caused him to look a little like someone who had crawled out of a dumpster. He placed his face in his hands and rubbed slowly. "Rubbing your face makes you feel a little better," he said, slightly chuckling.

Bobby laughed.

"I guess I know, Bobby. Hell, I was close to cracking more than once," he said, answering Bobby's, "you know how it is," question.

"Everybody does, but most people won't admit it. The streets are littered with guys who have checked out," Bobby said.

"I still need to work." Owen said as he rose from the bench. He gave Bobby a feeble salute. "Thanks, Lieutenant Blankenship."

Bobby saluted back. "Thank you, Lieutenant Black. Thank you for your service to our country."

Owen was getting into his pickup truck when Bobby's face brightened. He called after him. He invited him inside where he made Owen a proposition. His brother had a small construction business that seemed to be thriving since he had also returned from his service in Afghanistan. He had become proficient in advertising on the web and was taking business from all over Kentucky and neighboring states. He had to travel but that was the price of starting a new business. You took work wherever you found it. In the process there were strange offers that sometimes left him scratching his head. One of those offers was to work in Washington D.C. tearing down old buildings that somehow had gotten into historic districts where they didn't belong. They were usually small and crowded between other historic structures that could not be disturbed. Sometimes when they were salvageable he was asked to move them to other locations and structurally restore them. The major problem with taking on such an assignment was that no heavy equipment could be used, no wrecking balls, or buckets, jackhammers or anything that might cause vibrations. The theory was that damage might occur to structures nearby like brick walls and sensitive floor and ceiling joist. Everything had to be done by hand. It was a good job for college kids on break, or people who were down on their luck. Bobby's brother was non-union, but for this job he was willing to pay D.C. union scale, and that was pretty good money for pulling nails and loading loose lumber onto flatbed trucks. The problem for his brother was that he didn't have anyone who would work a temporary job that far from home.

"I'll take it. "Owen interrupted. "I guess it's better than holding a cardboard sign on my chest saying I'll work for food."

Bobby laughed for the second time, neither of them knowing that life would never be the same for Owen from that moment on. It was a watershed moment for Owen.

Chapter Five

On April 14th 1865, the dogwoods were in bloom, green grass was flourishing under blue skies, and cherry trees blossomed throughout Washington, D.C. The city was alive with activity as people celebrated the end of the Civil War. The country had gone through hell, but now everything was going to be alright. Old honest Abe had a handle on it.

On that day President Lincoln invited General Ulysses S. Grant to join him at Ford's Theatre for a presentation of Our American Cousin. He also invited Secretary of War, Edwin Stanton. Stanton met with General Grant at 3:00 p.m. to learn that Grant would be taking an early train out of Washington and was declining the President's offer. Stanton also declined after learning General Grant was not attending.

As the day progressed a light fog settled upon the city, turning what had been a very pleasant afternoon into a dreary curtain call on the most infamous day in American history. John Wilkes Booth was busy bandying about the city, enraged that Robert E. Lee had surrendered at Appomattox. He was incensed that the tyrant, Abraham Lincoln had won the civil war. Lee had surrendered but the war was not over for Booth. He had assembled a team to kidnap the President and negotiate a better outcome than reunification, but the logistics in doing that had made it impossible. Now he was intent on murdering him. Booth truly believed he would be hailed as a hero and the south would be inspired to rekindle the battle to secede from the north and the Confederacy would survive.

Booth never intended to overthrow the union government. His plan was to kill Lincoln, Vice President Andrew Johnson, and Secretary of State, William Seward, then escape to the south where he would be greeted with open arms. He only needed to have access to Lincoln, and the means to escape. He was well-funded, and his support team was ready to go at a moment's notice. The escape route had already been planned. He would flee across the Navy Yard Bridge.

It's unclear how Booth knew Lincoln was attending Ford's Theatre, or that he would be able to get to the President, but it was apparent he did. It was also unusual that Lincoln's bodyguard had left the President unattended and was getting drunk. He was never prosecuted for abandoning his post. The movement of Booth's co-conspirators were well-coordinated, but in some cases cold feet prevented them from achieving their objective. Booth's horse was left unattended, creating confusion, and a delay in fleeing. Andrew Johnson was left unscathed due to his assailant backing out at the last moment. William Seward was bludgeoned and stabbed, but he survived. The President was the only fatality, and it was at the hands of Booth.

Edwin Stanton was a very thinned-skinned argumentative little man who was puffed up on power and demanded things on his own terms. He was supportive of the war and reunification, but he was at odds with Lincoln about how the south would be treated in reconstruction. Lincoln wanted to let the rebels keep their guns and horses to return to their homes unmolested. The only requirement was to swear allegiance to the United States. Stanton wanted them punished and severely restricted. Lincoln was willing to allow the Virginia Legislature to convene with the same representatives who were there when they voted to secede. Stanton was outraged at the prospect, convinced Lincoln would be just as lenient to all other traitors. Stanton called Lincoln a baboon and an incompetent to other cabinet members on more than one occasion. On the very day the assassination was committed Stanton and Lincoln were in a disagreement regarding the Virginia Legislature.

Edwin Stanton as Secretary of War was second in line to the Presidency during that time in history, with only the Vice President proceeding him in succession. Strangely, Stanton was not a target of the conspiracy. Had every aspect succeeded Edwin Stanton would have been president.

Booth shot President Lincoln in the back of his head and jumped onto the stage of Ford's Theatre interrupting the presentation. He shouted," Sic semper tyrannis!" When he hit the floor his left leg was broken but he still managed to escape.

Lincoln's body was still warm when Stanton took control of the investigation, declaring Marshall Law and calling in the military. He also called in Lafayette Baker. Baker arrived on April 16th, one day after President Lincoln died. He immediately began rounding up the conspirators with such speed that it was only reasonable to conclude that he knew where they were beforehand.

Stanton had closed every bridge and road in the city except one, the Navy Yard Bridge. Booth took the Navy Yard Bridge and fled into Virginia, seemingly knowing it was the only way out. Baker was informed to find Booth and kill him. He was also instructed to retrieve his diary. Baker took possession of the diary in the company of Colonel Everton Conger. Baker read the diary carefully, and both he and Conger counted every page in the diary, and Baker insisted that Conger accompany him to deliver the diary to Stanton.

Later Baker claimed publicly, and in a book, that there were 18 missing pages. In 2015, a hundred and fifty years later those pages have never been recovered.

Chapter Six

Owen Black had never been to the U.S. Capitol. He had been in various airports in and around the large cities on the east coast while he was in service, but airports all looked the same to him, so it was all new when he arrived in Washington D.C. He had his military duffle bag slung over his shoulder packed with everything he thought he would need. He had never felt more alone in his life. He took a tour bus from the Library of Congress, and made the trek to all the D.C. monuments. When he arrived at the Korean War Veterans Monument, he was overcome with a feeling of dread. He knew little about the Korean War, or how the battles were conducted. It was nothing like the middle east, but there was something eerie about those soldiers advancing towards some unknown force as though they were rising out of the ground headed into oblivion, unknown, unappreciated, and gone. Never to be missed or thought of again. He wondered if his generation of fighters would go into that same vast conveyance of irrelevance. Owen was underwhelmed by D.C. He should have been in awe as he walked among the granite statues and the stone repositories of history's greatest leaders, but it seemed mundane and meaningless. He was unmoved as he stood at the feet of Abraham Lincoln as cell phones clicked and people milled around in silent respect for America's greatest President. Owen was empty. He had given the best part of his life to the military. He had killed people and broken things, and now he was like those statues of the Korean War Memorial. He was rising out of the ground headed for some unknown destiny to fade into oblivion.

Wilson Construction had acquired a room for Owen in a neighborhood in D.C. where he would be staying at the expense of the company. It wasn't a poor neighborhood, but it was a poor street. Most of the homes and apartments nearby were middle class and converted condos. The lofts were high-end accommodations. Owens place wasn't. It was a dump, and probably not long for the world. He was on the third level of a small brick building where stairs zig-zagged to each level with an apartment on each side. The stairway was completely enclosed without a single window. The building was dark and dreary; as gloomy as a medieval dungeon. The smell of mildew permeated the air, heavy and unhealthy to breath. Owen's residence wasn't an apartment, it was a room. There was a bathroom across the hallway to be shared with other residents. The only saving grace was that it had a window where the Capitol was visible in the distance.

Owen lugged the duffle bag as the stairs creaked with every step. He thought it might not be long before he was taking his prybar and hammer to the very place where he would be living. When he reached the third level he fished for his keys as he balanced the duffle bag on his shoulder. As he inserted the key, a voice came from inside. "Who is it?"

Surprised, Owen pulled back they key. The door creaked open revealing a chubby twenty something young man. "Are you Owen Black?" he asked. Owen was puzzled. His brow furrowed. "Yes, who are you?"

"I'm Bradley Sweeney. I'm your roommate," he said. Bradley was about five feet eleven, black hair, and weighed in at two hundred and forty pounds. His face was round bearing large brown eyes and dark bushy eyebrows. Other than being fat he might pass for Owen's son under the right conditions. Owen's hair was very dark with gray streaks, he was five eleven and had busy eyebrows. The difference was that Owen was as fit as a college athlete.

Owen looked around the room. The dingy green walls were free of decoration, the floor was a tongue and groove dry pine. The window revealing the U.S. Capitol in the distance was bare of window dressings, the ceiling had a stain from where it had leaked. It was just as he remembered when he had looked at it earlier in the week. The only difference was the full-sized bed was gone and now there were two singles and a used chest of drawers instead. "What the fuck," Owen said, dropping his duffle onto the floor.

"I'm your roommate," Bradley said timidly, turning his palms out.

It was evident that the company was trying to keep costs under control but putting him in a run down, mildew-laden one room apartment should have been bad enough, but now he had a roommate. Anger shot through him in an instant, but quickly he drew in his horns. Bradley Sweeney was looking at Owen with an apologetic expression. It wasn't his fault they would be crammed together like sardines, but he looked as guilty as if he had made the arrangements himself.

Owen sighed. "Sorry, I know this isn't your fault, but this isn't what I thought it was going to be."

Bradley didn't know anything about Owen. Owen could only presume the kid thought he was some guy who was down on his luck; a loser taking a temporary job when he was pushing forty. Other than having a military retirement, and a duffle bag, the presumption wasn't that far off.

After several minutes, the conversation between them became less strained. Owen found Bradley to be a polite, quiet young man who was floundering to find himself. He had flunked out of college and now was just living day to day. His father, a PhD, who was assistant curator at Albemarle Charlottesville Historical Society. His mother was dead. Bradley was adopted and by every measure he was a disappointment to his father. Bradly was so uncomfortable living with his father that he answered an ad on the internet to work with a demolition team there in D.C. Neither Owen nor Bradley knew when they took the job that they were the demolition team. Two guys with hammers and prybars. Bradley would have taken anything just to get away from his father and by the looks of it, "anything," was the proper definition. Owen and Bradley were both at a crossroads in their lives.

It was a cool September morning in Washington D.C. Cars and trucks as far away as Pennsylvania Avenue could be heard making their way around the city. Owen was accustomed to Leesville, Kentucky where it was as quiet as a graveyard at four in the morning, so the sounds of the city had kept him up. Bradley Sweeney was still sleeping. Owen looked at him for a moment, shook his head and bit his lower lip. He had to remind himself that Bradley wasn't at fault for the accommodations. Owen wasn't guilty of anything either. He had fought for his country, he was faithful to his wife, and lost his job only because the plant had closed. "It is what it is," he said to himself, swatting away the negative thoughts trying to get embedded in his mind. He opened the door leaving Bradley sleeping.

Four thirty a.m. was early for anyone no matter where you were so when he hit the streets they were deserted. He wondered where all the vehicle noise had come from during the night. He could still hear trucks accelerating, and brakes squeaking coming from somewhere, but he couldn't see them. He walked about ten blocks to the Starbucks he had seen across the street from the Library of Congress where he caught the tour bus.

A cup of coffee was four dollars ninety-five cents plus tax. At the Casey's General Store back home coffee was eighty-nine cents. Obviously, he was going to have to find a cheaper place for coffee or learn to live without it. The Starbucks was a little one room operation with oil floors, a counter and tables to accommodate less than a dozen people. It looked like something you would find in downtown St. Louis or Memphis. There was a man and woman eating an egg and bagel and having a caramel macchiato who were the only patrons there. It didn't look at all appealing, but it probably cost as much as a week's groceries for some people. It was five a.m. Traffic was beginning to pick up on Pennsylvania Avenue, tour buses were lining up and idling on the curbside. Life in Washington, D.C. was about to begin for Owen. He walked back to his apartment. Bradley Sweeney was still sleeping, curled up in a fetal position. They were scheduled to meet one of the company men to get tools and brief instructions. Tearing down little shabby buildings didn't require a lot of engineering skill, but they at least had to know some of the details.

Bradley came to life not long after Owen's return. His eyes were like two large red marbles as he sluggishly milled about the room trying to get himself into gear. It was easy to see that he wasn't accustomed to walking around in the bright light of early morning. The t-shirt he had slept in was riding up exposing his round white belly. He was walking on the left leg of his sweatpants and the right leg had ridden up past his knee. To keep things in perspective Owen had to run the phrase over in his mind, "It is what it is." He had been in close quarters while in the military and it seemed so natural, but now it was unsettling. He would have to adjust.

When they arrived at their work site a guy in work clothes and a yellow safety hat was waiting. There were flatbed wagons resembling farm wagons, and a humongous dumpster parked in the alley. The guy's instructions were, "just start tearing it down. Put the lumber on the flatbeds and the junk in the dumpster." In five minutes he was gone.

And so they began. Starting on the rooftop, peeling off shingles, working their way to the rafters and walls, they sweated through the day. When they were done they went back to their room and waited for the shower to be vacated by other residents. It was like that every day throughout September and into October. They found a check in their mailbox each Friday and they ate dinner at Warburton's Bar and Grill. Bradley had lost twenty-five pounds. His body was lean and his face no longer round and pudgy. He was a nice-looking kid. He bought a coffee pot and mounted some pictures on the wall above his bed. In the beginning Bradley left empty soft drink bottles and wrappers lying around, his bed was never made, and books were stacked on the floor. As time passed Owen's presence had an effect on him and he began picking up after himself. He learned how to make his bed in a tight military style, and he was up and ready to go by morning light. He had become a different person than the kid Owen found in the room that afternoon in September. Owen was different too. This was the first time in his life when he wasn't under the influence of others. He and Susan were a couple starting from eighth grade on and then onto the military before the ink was dry on his high-school diploma. He and Susan were married while she was in college and he between deployments. After he was discharged he worked in the factory providing for his family. In his thirty-eight years this was the first time he was actually completely on his own. Not having Susan and the girls had left a hole in him but something was happening to him that he had not expected; he was becoming completely carefree. He was making union scale, so he had plenty of money to send back home. There were days when Iraq, Afghanistan, or Syria, never entered his mind. Bradley Sweeney turned out to be a blessing. He was still shy and introverted, but he liked Owen, and their relationship was tight. What Owen didn't know was that fate was about to put a wrinkle into everything.

Early in November the building at 17th Street was gone. Piece by piece the structure was dismantled until there was nothing left but a muddy hole in the ground. Each week flatbeds with the lumber were taken out along with a change in dumpsters. Now the area was just as uppity as the rest of the neighborhood.

 The man in the yellow safety hat was back with a new assignment. Owen was relieved. He was worried that his employment might have come to an end as the last of the debris was hauled away. He knew he would have to find a real job in the future but at the moment making old buildings disappear was good enough. Their new location was close to the U.S Capitol two blocks off Pennsylvania. It was a three-story brick; only eleven feet wide, abutting two other structures. Edmondson was a busy street with shops, restaurants, and upscale retail establishments. Most were from the civil war era and required a permit to make improvements or changes. The front of the building had to remain in its original state, and the interior had to be done in a manner acceptable to D.C. historical standards. The façade would be cleaned, fake windows installed for aesthetic purposes and the interior taken down to bare studs. It was their job to gut the building and clean up the junk with as little notice as possible. The reconstruction would be done by specialist. They adjusted quickly to their new assignment. It was dusty and dry but it was a blessing to be out of the weather. All along Edmondson Street it was alive with activity, customers and clients busily being separated from their money.

Owen and Bradley were invisible as they scraped away decaying plastered walls layer by layer until nothing was left but bare rough-hewn studs that had not been exposed for a hundred and fifty years. Bradley was inside a closet stirring up dust and banging robustly against anything left hanging or in his way. He had become a wrecking machine. Owen was shoveling whatever came out into a portable dumpster when Bradley pitched out a brown leather satchel. When it hit the floor, it looked like a flower bag falling from the highest shelf in the grocery store. After the dust cleared Owen picked it up, blew more dust from it in order to see it better. The force of hitting the floor had cracked the leather exposing the silk lining. Owen pitched it aside to resume his work. They had found numerous interesting things inside the walls at 1543 Edmondson Street including a metal whisky flask, planer knives, two pouches of nails, a carving stating SIMON 1864 and one carving by John proclaiming his love for Sarah. They were careful not to disfigure the inscriptions, leaving them as much like they were found as possible. Everything they found was interesting, but the satchel seemed the most intriguing. A satchel left to be enclosed behind those walls might contain gold or silver or nothing at all.

At 5:00 p.m. Owen put the satchel behind the seat of his 150 for later examination. He and Bradley decided to hit Warburton's Bar and Grill on their way in. They were acquainted with a few of the regulars and the bartenders and waitresses knew them. Before they even sat down Owen knew there was something different. Four young men at the end of the bar were standing, loud talking over each other and laughing. T-shirts and designer jeans were worn to accentuate hard bodies bulging with muscles. They were chiseled. The aroma of sausages and hamburgers on the grill could not overcome the odor of cologne in the air. The words "Gym Rat" was prominently across one man's chest while another was wearing "No Pain No Gain" on his back. They were belligerent. More than likely they were different when they weren't together but in a pack they would always exhibit bravado trying to one up each other. Three of the four would usually stay between the lines limiting their actions to acceptable behavior but there was always one who would be aggressive, ready to push the outside of the envelope. Owen had already honed in on him. His shirt read, "No Fear." He also knew the three others would follow him. Owen's gut was telling him to turn around and head out the door, but Bradley had already signaled to Chloe, a smiling waitress who was bringing their usual draft beers. She had perked up when she saw Bradley entering and hurried to be the one to serve them. He wasn't the same fat kid who had his first draft been in that bar. He was still shy, but he looked rugged and strong. His personality was still the same, quiet, introverted and polite. Working with his bare hands had turned him into a rock. That look and his quiet mannerisms were a magnet to women. He just didn't know it.

When Chloe rounded the bar passing the four fitness buffs, No Fear grabbed her elbow causing the beer to splash out onto the tray. "Hey, baby, where ya going," he asked. She flashed a disapproving glance as she settled her tray, still moving away from him. "Come back when you're done, I've got a question." After she walked away the other three laughed. Gym Rate covered his mouth and giggled like a fool.

Even after being grabbed Chloe was all smiles when she approached Bradley and Owen. "Hello, Brad," she smiled. Bradley said, "Hi." He had no idea she was giving that look.

The one every guy wants to get from a good-looking woman. But still even Chloe didn't realize it. It radiated from her but it was so natural that it unconsciously bubbled to the surface. Owen chuckled to himself, "Bradley doesn't even get it," he thought.

No Fear was watching through bloodshot eyes. Resentment was plastered all over his face. Chloe served two other customers and then she was back. No Fear had stopped talking to his buddies, he was shifting his weight back and forth impatiently. The others were still laughing like hyenas, but No Fear looked as though he had sucked a lemon.

Bradley was quiet as Chloe chirped on about celebrities and congressmen who had occupied that very same table where he was sitting. When she asked Bradley questions his replies were usually as long as yes or no, but sometimes he just gawked at her stifled for an answer. He was finally starting to get it that she was flirting with him, but that prospect made him as nervous as if someone had a razor- sharp knife to his throat. Owen was amused. It was heartwarming to see someone his age so innocent.

It didn't have the same effect on No Fear. He was pacing, several times walking past them trying to make eye contact without results only to return to his friends who were getting louder by the minute. Finally, No Fear walked up behind Chloe and stood uncomfortably close. "Hey, baby, I thought we were gonna talk."

Chloe's eyebrows raised. "No," she said. No Fear's lower jaw muscles were tight as his brow furrowed. "You've been with these two fucks long enough," he growled. Owen's expression never changed as he pushed his chair away from the table. No Fear stepped back and said, "Where you going asshole."

Bradley's eyes were like saucers. He had never been in a heated argument. Getting into a bar fight was as likely as going to Mars. Chloe signaled for the bartender. In a moment the bartender and another man were standing at her elbow. No Fear's friends had taken notice and were gathered behind him. "Buddy, you and your friends need to find another watering hole."

Owen rose from his chair and said, "It's okay, we're leaving," knowing Chole was in safe hands. No Fear chuckled. "Chicken shit," he said as Owen walked away. Bradley followed him meekly.

It was dark outside. Some of the shops were closed but the restaurants and bars were glowing soft yellow lights. Some of them had discreet neon signage acceptable to D.C.'s strict standards. A dull vanilla glow glistened off the brick pavers and shadows were cast along the street by planters containing pink foliage and boxwood. It was the last place on earth to find someone looking for a fight. Owen was just stepping into the alley to head for the parking lot when he heard No Fear crowing like a rooster. Gym Rate joined in clucking and giggling. Bradley stopped and turned around. "Just leave us alone, please," he said. Owen stopped too. Bradley noticed Owen's hand trembling. His eyes were fixed on No Fear. The loud- mouth kept advancing towards them. "The man said to leave us alone," Owen barked. No Fear saw Owen's hand shaking. "What are you gonna do, chicken shit, piss your pants."

Owen took two steps towards him. No Fear continued to advance. He puffed up his chest and flexed his muscles. At that point Owen stepped into him. In just a flash he reached across his body grabbing No Fear's right elbow, simultaneously covering his right hand with No Fears thumb in his palm. In one quick movement No Fear's body was slammed to the ground. With the quickness and grace of an Olympic gymnast his right foot came down on No Fear's ribs with a thud, and then a second kick followed. No Fear was gasping but he wasn't moving. Owen glared at the other three with contempt shining in his eyes. They stood with their mouths open. They had never seen that intensity in someone's eyes in the local gym. Bradley was so stunned that he couldn't move.

"You can come and get this piece of shit, or you can get some of what he got. It's up to you," Owen said, still glaring at them. The muscle heads cautiously advanced to retrieve No Fear. By then he was able to breathe in short panicked gasps. He most likely had broken ribs and a bruised lung that would require a visit to the emergency room.

"If you sonofbitches call the police, I'll kill all three of you." Owen warned. Bradley was watching him as though he had seen something drop in from outer space. In his twenty-one years he had never seen anything like it.

As they walked through the alley to the parking lot guilt was creeping into Owen's thoughts. Bradley was silent. Owen wanted to get into his mind to know what he was thinking. Was he terrified by what he had seen? Had he lost all respect for him? Owen had done things that he couldn't believe himself and this was small by comparison, but it felt wrong.

It was a quiet ride back to the room. Owen had forgotten about the satchel riding behind the seat. When they were back in the room Owen finally broke the silence. "Bradley, I'm sorry about what happened back there."

Bradley stared at the wall. He was rolling over in his mind what had happened. Owen was prepared for whatever Bradley's reaction might be. Finally, he said, "That was pretty violent. I'm sure it was illegal in some aspect but that dude was asking for it. I don't know if it was right, or necessary, but to tell you the truth I was kind of proud of you." Owen sighed and then chuckled. "Okay," he said, and that was the end of it.

Chapter Seven

It was two days before Owen remembered leaving the leather satchel behind his truck seat. When he retrieved it he found it to be fragile, crumbling in places with the lining shining through. There was a small steel clasp holding the leather strap with an oval shaped nut on both ends. It had corroded making it impossible to open without destroying the clasp. Owen looked at it, then Bradley took his turn. They discussed breaking the clasp. Bradley thought it might be a valuable relic and should be left in its original condition. They agreed to lay it aside. Bradley read "Of Mice and Men," for the fourth time since they had been there. Owen listened to Van Morrison on his ancient Walkman. In less than an hour both of them had picked up the satchel, blew more dust from it, turned it from side to side to examine, and then returned it to the chest of drawers.

Bradley fetched a bottle of leather restoration oil from his suitcase where it was stashed behind his bed. He carefully applied the oil to the satchel, rubbing it until it was as smooth as silk. When he finished there was a small engraving on the flap exposing the name, Edwin Stanton. A serious expression settled on Bradley's face. He held the satchel up for Owen to read it.

"I guess it was Edwin Stanton's. He won't need it now," Owen said facetiously.

Bradley grunted.

"What does that mean, that grunt?" Owen said. Bradley ran his hand through his hair. "I wasn't a history major, but I think Edwin Stanton was Abraham Lincoln's Secretary of War."

"There must be a lot of Edwin Stantons in the world," Owen said.

"It's been in that wall since the Civil War." Bradley said.

"That's a stretch," Owen said.

"You're right, it is. I mean what are the chances?"

"If we had a computer we could look it up," Owen said.

"I've got a computer," Bradley said.

"You've got computer? You've read Of Mice and Men twenty times since we've been here and you have a computer somewhere" Owen gasped.

"I've read Of Mice and Men four times since we've been here." Bradley objected. Owen chuckled in disbelief.

"I hate social media. All the negative stuff being said bugs me. I don't want to be involved." Bradley said.

"But you have a computer?"

"Yes. It's old but it works."

Once the computer was retrieved and the battery charged Owen researched everything he could find on the web pertaining to Edwin Stanton. It was interesting. He couldn't believe so much history was left out of his high school classes. "*Now he belongs to the ages*," was the fabled words uttered by Stanton at Lincoln's deathbed. He had seen that phrase engraved over Abraham Lincoln's memorial in Springfield, Illinois where he was buried, but had no idea where it came from. Outside of that there were few positive references on the internet about Stanton. Several conspiracies suggested Stanton was involved in Lincoln's assassination, and others argued that those conspiracies theories were little more than speculation. In one of the articles John Wilkes Booth's diary was discussed in depth. Eighteen pages mysteriously disappeared while it was in Stanton's possession. That was the article Owen keyed in on.

It was all interesting, but that still didn't mean anything. The satchel might have belonged to Edwin Stanton the butcher, or Edwin Stanton the livery driver, or any number of Edwin Stantons, but it was intriguing to think they had Secretary of War, Edwin Stanton's satchel in their possession. Neither Owen nor Bradley were ready to accept conspiracy theories, but it was suspicious to find something like that enclosed behind a plastered wall. At that point they decided not to open the satchel but to sleep on it.

The next day Owen and Bradley went back to work. The incident with the four muscle heads seemed so long ago that it was nearly forgotten. However, the satchel was still on Owen's mind. Bradley was thinking about it too, but he was hard to read-he held his emotions close to his chest. Owen didn't know how to get into Bradley's head. During their lunch break they talked about the satchel and decided they would break into it to find out what was inside.

It was spitting snow as Owen gazed out the window into the gray clouds on the horizon. The Capitol dome was nearly invisible in the distance fading into an endless blur of flurries and thick dark clouds. All those articles Owen had read were swirling around in his thoughts. Everything in society these days was sensationalized, but he also knew anything was possible. Would they find something incriminating inside that fragile leather pouch? Would there be eighteen pages of a diary of the most reviled murderer in American history? Would Edwin Stanton be capable of committing treason? History was full of men who murdered others for power. Hitler tortured and killed six million Jews, and there are Chinese bodies by the millions in mass graves to give Chairman Mao total control of China. Watching the Capitol dome in the distance Owen suspected there were as many criminals routed through there as there were honest men, so why would it be hard to believe that one little power-hungry politician in 1865 would be exempt from suspicion. Or was his mind simply just running away with him. That satchel probably had nothing noteworthy inside. Still he couldn't wait to break it open to find out.

Bradley was quietly watching Owen as he placed the satchel on the chest of drawers. With a channel lock pliers and screwdriver Owen worked methodically and in moments the strap was free and the flap folder open. He was careful as he spread the sides to look. There were several time yellowed sheets exposed. Owen left them inside carefully thumbing through them counting out eighteen pieces. His heart was pounding. It was strange. Opening the door to a concrete bunker with possible Al Quaeda inside had caused his heart to pound and his blood to rush through his veins like a freight train, and now here he was with a flimsy leather folder in his hand and it was creating the same result. He swallowed hard. "This is it, Bradley. There's eighteen pages!" Owen looked up to see a distressed expression on Bradley's face. "Don't take them out, Owen," he said in a strained voice. A voice Owen had never heard before. "It could change history, Owen. It's sacrilegious."

"It may not be anything, Bradley. Maybe it's not even the same guy," Owen said.

"Edwin Stanton's satchel with eighteen pages in it – it's too coincidental! We shouldn't open it."

Owen studied Bradley's face. He was serious. He knew Bradley was a stand-up guy. He didn't spout his opinions all the time, or at all, but Owen suspected there were lines he wouldn't cross. Owen had crossed many forbidden lines in his life, and the burden was a heavy load to tow. Now he wanted to pull those pages from that satchel and read every word, but he would wait until Bradley was ready. They had found it together; they would open it together no matter how ridiculous Bradley's argument was.

Chapter Eight

At three a.m., Owen was dreaming about Susan and the girls. They were at the company picnic. The clown who had been twisting balloon animals was trying to urge Owen into being part of the act. He grabbed Owen by the shoulder trying to get him to center stage. He opened his eyes to find Bradley shaking him. "What the hell," Owen said.

"I've got a suggestion," Bradley whispered as though there were someone else in the room that he didn't want to hear. Owen glanced at the clock.

"We can take out the last page and look at it," Bradley said.

"It's three a.m."

"Oh, I'm sorry I woke you. It can wait," Bradley said apologetically.

Owen sat up and rubbed his face. "Okay, let's do it, but what will that prove?"

"Most things like that don't have the really heavy stuff at the end, but we should have enough to authenticate it. Something that won't change the course of history," he whispered. "We can get a flashlight, and take a look," he added.

"Why would we need a flashlight? Owen said as he flipped on the light. "And you can stop whispering."

Owen fetched the satchel and carefully spread open the flap. He separated the pages and took out the last one carefully. There were only five words at the top of the page. It said, *"Another stain on the old banner." Jwb*.

Chapter Nine

Owen and Bradley were as stunned by that final page in the satchel as finding a 1943 copper penny in the ashtray of the 150. Was it too far out to believe they had speculated on the contents, and lo and behold, that was exactly what they had found? Owen suggested that maybe they were being hoaxed. Was there a hidden camera somewhere in the ceiling, and would there be a laughing commentator coming out of the closet with a microphone in his hand?

That last entry and the initials were as much as hitting a nail right on the head. *"Another stain on the old banner,"* were the last words John Wilkes Booth spoke before he went into the abyss, but It still wasn't confirmation when you considered every other possibility. Someone could have been making notes, or writing a news story about the assassination, or any number of things, but being in Edwin Stanton's satchel and contained within a hundred and fifty year old wall narrowed the chances.

The only way to know was to find someone to authenticate the writing. In addition to Bradley having a computer, he had another surprise for Owen. His father was the Assistant Curator at the Albemarle Charlottesville Historical Society. He had a PhD in art, history and archeology. He would probably know by just looking if the writing was similar to

Booth's, and he would have the means to authenticate the writing and verify the year the paper was produced. What Bradley didn't say was that Arthur Sweeney was a sarcastic, bitter man who thought he should be curator at the Met in New York City instead of a local history bin. Along with that the Curator in Charlottesville had a Bachelor's degree and Arthur thought it was totally beneath him to answer to someone so far beneath him. He insisted that the Curator address him as Dr. Sweeney. Arthur Sweeney was so arrogant and condescending that being around him for more than ten minutes would suffice for a lifetime. Lack of brilliance was never an obstacle for Arthur Sweeney. He was brilliant but nobody wanted to work with him or for him. Alcohol and gambling were his way of coping rather than changing his approach to others. He was often drunk bloviating about his credentials to anyone who would listen. He and his wife, Wendy, adopted Bradley when he was three years old. Bradley was invisible to him even as a child. Wendy died when Bradley was thirteen and from that point forward Bradley was no more than a burden. Bradley was a straight -A- student at IMG Elementary school and an honors student at Oak Hill Boarding School. He was accepted at the University of Virginia but flunked out after two semesters. Bradley's failure had nothing to do with his ability to handle the load. He just stopped going to classes and never made excuses for his demise, but that was his way. Arthur needed to validate his own status by spouting about having a student at The University of Virginia, but whatever benefit it was to Bradley wasn't a consideration.

Bradley hated asking his father for anything but this thing with the Edwin Stanton satchel was compelling. Owen

Black was Bradley's only friend, and since they were in this together. It had more meaning to him than anything had in a long time. With that in mind, he suggested they visit Arthur Sweeney and ask for his assistance.

They finished their work week before starting the two-hour drive from Washington, D.C., to Charlottesville.   They didn't leave until Saturday afternoon which seemed odd to Owen. He wanted to get right to it but Bradley insisted on leaving after lunch. What Bradley didn't say was that Arthur would be sleeping all morning after being drunk all night gambling on the internet.

As they drove Bradley looked out the window, his thoughts meandering deeper into his past life. The Berkshires along I-95 were covered with a light frosting reminiscent of James Taylors "Sweet Baby James." Owen could feel the tension in the air as Bradley sat forward in the seat like a child waiting for a scolding.

Finally Owen broke the silence. "Bradley, I don't really know much about you. I mean about your family and all, but we're friends, right? Will this put you in a bad light? I mean, we'll have to be discreet about what we have here."

 Bradley didn't answer immediately. He looked even more uncomfortable than he had before. "I don't know much about you either, Owen," he said, obviously diverting the question.

"There's a lot of things about me you don't want to know, Brad." Owen said, uneasily. This was as deep as they had ever come to having a sensitive conversation about their relationship.

"Are you ashamed of your past?"

Owen waited for a long moment, his face conveying that he was in deep thought, and then he said, "No. I went into the military because I wanted to see the world. Special services was more of a challenge than anything else. In the end I was fighting to survive. I killed people trying not to be killed. I'm not ashamed but it haunts me."

"I think you're a good man, Owen," Bradley said. After another long pause Bradley said, "I'm ashamed of myself but I don't know why. I haven't committed any crimes and I've never deliberately hurt anyone. I just feel like I've let everybody down."

"Because you flunked out of college?"

"No, it's because I'm fat, I'm too stupid to have a conversation, and I'm adopted."

Owen sighed, "Brad, you're not fat. You're in military grade condition. You don't talk a lot, but some people think that's a good thing."

"My dad never introduced me to his friends without somehow getting around to telling them I was adopted. That kind of makes you feel like there's something wrong with you."

"You know that's not true, don't you?"

"I do but it sort of gets ingrained into you."

"I think you're a good man too, Bradley. I'm glad they put us together."

The conversation ended on that note.

The subdivision in Charlottesville where Arthur Sweeney lived was an upscale community, beautiful homes, expensive landscaping and traffic calming round-abouts. Arthur's house was as expensive as any of the others but the grass was shabby looking, the windows were dirty, and the landscaping badly in need of trimming. A note was taped to the front door from the homeowners' association that citations would be issued if immediate action was not taken to correct the situation. Bradley removed it, keeping it in his hand as he pressed the doorbell. A tall thin man with gray hair, gray stubble, wearing a robe and house-shoes answered the door. He gave them a puzzled look and said, "May I help you?"

Bradley handed the warning to him. He looked at Bradley blankly for a moment, then gasped. "Bradley, my lord, you look different!"

"I've lost a little weight," Bradley said.

"I would say so. You look almost respectable. Who is your companion, Bradley?" he asked.

"Owen Black – Owen, this is my father."

Arthur extended his hand. "I'm Dr. Sweeney," he said. Owen shook his hand, noting the smell of alcohol on his breath. Inside it was dark, the shades pulled tight blocking the light. An odor in the air similar to that of a nursing home was present. Inside there were mountains of books and magazines strewn about, expensive furniture supporting piles of newspapers, a violin, and a saxophone were lying on the floor. The place was untidy from the front door throughout the house. The conversation was immediately uncomfortable to the point that Arthur asked Bradley at least twice how he was doing. Bradley's answer was, "Fine."

Arthur went to the wine bar, picked up a glass, wiped it with a towel then poured a glass of pinot noir. He didn't bother offering anything to Bradley or Owen. He swirled the wine in the glass, cupped his hands around the rim and sniffed. There was a revealing gaze of disapproval in Bradley's eyes. The gesture of sniffing the wine was as useless as garland on a one-thousand-dollar plate dinner in an effort to dress up two ounces of veal. Arthur had drunk enough wine from that cabinet to know the aroma and taste of every drop in every bottle. His swirling and sniffing was nothing more than show.

"I don't have beer," Arthur said glancing at Owen, his nose slightly elevated. It was a move he had perfected. Walking around with your nose in the air was an adage Arthur had no problem with. Owen scanned the room, resting his gaze on a paper plate that appeared to have been sitting there until it was curled stiffly upward, and then moving on to the newspapers left on the couch, finally to a saucer with a half-eaten doughnut. "Two can play that game," he thought, taking a swift sniff, tilting his head back so slightly.

"Bradley doesn't drink wine," Arthur said. He glanced at him. Bradley was up walking towards the dining room. "What happened to the maid, Dad? Is she sick?"

Arthur ignored the question. "I think Bradley should have learned to appreciate good wine as I did. It's off putting to attend a special engagement and your social graces are so lacking that you cannot even recognize a port from a vignoles."

"Mom's crystal is covered with dust," Bradley said.

"I can't be blamed for Bradley's lack of interest in the finer things in life. It's not in his DNA to follow my lead. He is my adopted son after all."

Owen was impatient. He walked to the crystal cabinet and eyeballed the dust Bradley had mentioned. "Dr. Sweeney, we have a problem. Bradley tells me that you're the assistant curator at Albemarle Charlottesville Historical Society."

"For now, yes." Arthur said, implying that a better gig was just around the corner.

"He also said you're qualified far beyond the position you currently occupy." Owen was trying to sound authoritative.

"Thank you, Bradley. You've stated the obvious, but I appreciate that you recognize it." Arthur said. His ego already oversized, was elevated.

"The point is – is that we have a document we need to have authenticated. Bradley thinks you have the skills to do that for us."

Arthur glanced at Bradley. A stone replica standing in the doorway to the dining room would have been less rigid than Bradley was at that moment. He wanted to apologize and walk out the door. Owen took the paper from the folder and handed it to Arthur. Arthur's eyes widened. "Those were the last words uttered by John Wilkes Booth before he was shot dead by Boston Corbet."

"He actually survived a short time before he died," Owen said, trying to sound informed. He knew not to say more. Sometimes knowing a little will make you sound more ignorant than you actually are.

"Of course," Arthur barked, "It was a fatal shot, however. Everybody knows that!"

Owen didn't answer. Arthur's eyes were glued to the writing. "The initials are jwb and the paper is Civil War grade. This may be something written by John Wilkes Booth, or someone writing about the assassination. There is no known inscription like this anywhere."

"Is it Booth's? Owen asked.

"I need to compare it with Booth's known handwriting. I have a computer program with all that kind of stuff available. It might take me two days to review it and come up with an opinion. Where did this come from?" Arthur asked.

"We think it's part of Booth's diary," Owen said. Bradley's eyes widened. He was standing behind Arthur waving his arms wildly, mouthing, "Nooo!"

Owen grimaced, knowing he had said too much. "I can't tell your where it came from. Not now anyway."

"Have you got other examples?"

"I can't discuss where we got it, or anything about it. Not right now," Owen said.

"I'll need it all in order to be thorough," Arthur said.

"Dad, it's not ours. We can't say anything about where we got it, or anything more than you already know. If you don't want to find out if it's authentic, we'll take it to the University history department on Monday. You don't have to do it."

"I'll do it," Arthur snapped. "I'll call you on your cell phone when I've finished."

"You've got a cell phone?" Owen asked raising his eyebrows.

"I've got one. It's not charged. It's in my suitcase."

Owen snorted softly.

After a short conversation Owen and Bradley were back on the road. Owen realized he had said too much. Bradley tried to smooth things over, stating that Arthur would have asked so many questions that eventually they would have had to have given up something. The problem was that Bradley didn't trust Arthur. If there was a way of stealing credit for uncovering something historical and valuable there were no lines he wouldn't cross. He felt uneasy about leaving that one sheet in his possession.

Chapter Ten

Two days passed without word from Arthur. Bradley didn't say he was worried but he frequently checked his cell phone to see if there was a message from Arthur. Being secluded in that room without communication had not bothered him before, and all during that time he had a cell phone in his suitcase and chosen not to use it, but now he was looking at the empty screen every twenty minutes. He didn't have to say he was worried, his actions were speaking louder than words.

That same evening Arthur Sweeney was visited by Robert Swag, an enforcer for an east coast gambling syndicate. He was a no-nonsense kind of guy who didn't mind breaking a few bones, or even burying a corpse in a cornfield – a corpse who assumed room temperature by his own hand – his idea of rounding off numbers. Arthur was into them for about ninety thousand and Swag was assigned to get it. He had been to visit Arthur on two previous occasions, but Arthur was yet to satisfy the terms Swag had given him. Contrary to popular opinion, the mob didn't kill pathetic losers like Arthur when they were in over their heads without at least giving them a payment plan. Getting money from them was the primary goal and it was hard to get money out of a dead man. If it became obvious that the debt would never be paid Swag didn't have a problem with putting a bullet into their heads either. He believed Arthur had already crossed that line.

When Swag arrived, he didn't bother knocking. He opened the front door and walked in. Sweeney was sitting at his computer studying the screen intensely. When he saw Swag he was so shocked that he jumped up knocking his chair over spilling wine onto a stack of papers lying on his desk.

"Why are you perpetually intruding upon my property? I've asked you not to do that!" Arthur snapped.

"Yeah, and I've asked you not to use any of them three syllable words on me neither."

"What do you want?"

"I want money, Arthur."

"I gave you a thousand dollars less than a month ago," Arthur said indignantly.

"The bosses want ten thousand," Swag said.

"I can't do that. It's impossible."

"You're gonna hafta-- you're gonna be lookin' at some bad luck, Arthur."

"Yes, and I may be going to the FBI to report you for extortion" Arthur glared at Swag. "And Mr. Swag, you can address me as Dr. Sweeney." He added.

Swag laughed. "Yeah, and I can see the headline in the paper, DR. SWEENEY local important somtin er another found with his head caved in. Funeral arrangements at a later date. - Oh, but wait a minute, you ain't gonna be have'n no funeral. It's gonna be you and a few squirrels out there in the woods."

Arthur sat back in his chair and ran his hand through his hair. "I'm onto something that might bring in a considerable amount of money, but I need time."

"What is it?" Swag asked.

"It's this," he said, holding the yellowed sheet of paper up for Swag to look at it.

"That ain't worth nothin!" Swag snorted.

"Have you ever heard of Don Mclean, Mr. Swag?"

"No, I ain't."

"How about" Bye, Bye Miss American Pie?"

"That's some kinda hippy song, but what's that gotta do with anything?"

"Well, Don Mclean sold the rough draft he made of that song for four and a half million dollars and this paper right here, if everything comes to fruition, is worth a hundred times more than "American Pie."

"Did he write that?"

"No." It's something historical. It's something they've been looking for, for a hundred and fifty years."

"What the fuck is it?" Swag asked, his impatience was showing on his face and in his voice. Swag was a man whose patience ran thin quickly.

"You wouldn't understand what it is or what makes it valuable." Arthur said.

"You can tell me or I'm gonna put a bullet in your head and take it," Swag demanded.

"It's a page from John Wilkes Booth's diary," Arthur stated quickly, knowing that Swag meant business.

"Who's that?" Swag spouted.

"The John Wilkes Booth who assassinated Abraham Lincoln."

"Oh, that John Wilkes Booth. I knew that," Swag said. "Wouldn't the Feds take that away from you?" He asked, showing more aptitude than Arthur had given him credit for.

"They would, but I would sell it on the black market - on the dark web, if you know what I mean."

"Why don't I take it and give it to my bosses and they can figure out what to do with it."

"No! Arthur shouted defiantly.

"Don't yell at me, Arthur, or shit's gonna go downhill in a hurry," Swag shouted back.

"First of all, there are seventeen additional pages. I'll have to get them before it becomes relevant. It has to be complete before I can put it out for auction."

Swag realized instantly that Arthur had a plan to get off the hot seat, and he was astute enough to know there would be more in it than a meager ninety thousand dollars. He also knew that Arthur wasn't about to share.

"Where are them other papers?" Swag said sternly, leaning forward glaring into Arthur's eyes. Arthur swallowed hard, knowing he was looking into the eyes of a murderer. When Swag leaned forward he knew he was in trouble. It wasn't a matter of getting rich, or wiping out his debt, it was now all about staying alive.

"I'm not gonna ask you again, Arthur. Where is the rest of it, and who's got it?"

Whatever backbone Arthur had vanished in an instant. His voice was quivering, his hands shaking violently. "My son has it. My adopted son and a man by the name of Owen Black."

Swag didn't say another word. His black eyes were bearing down on Arthur. "I don't know where he lives but I heard him say that he is staying in an apartment near Warburton's Bar and Grill in Washington, D.C."

Swag reached across Arthur's desk and retrieved the paper. Arthur was too frightened to stop him. He could hear Swag breathing, smell garlic on his breath. He was frozen stiff in his chair. When he felt the barrel of Swag's gun against the back of his head he whimpered like a frightened dog.

He didn't hear the blast. Blood gushed forward spattering on the computer screen, his eyes rolled back into their sockets and disappeared. Swag slipped the gun back into his coat and said, "Thank you, Dr. Sweeney. I'm gonna let myself out."

Chapter Eleven

Swag was a loyal soldier. The paper he had retrieved from Arthur Sweeney might have been worthless, or worth millions. He never once considered trying to broker it on his own. It would go directly to Carlos Triano, his boss. If it had any value the boss would find it and turn a profit. Still he was a little nervous about reporting in. Killing Sweeney wasn't exactly what he was instructed to do.

Triano's office was in the rear portion of Sorrento's Italian Ristorante in Little Italy. Getting to the boss' office was a grind. Swag's 1999 Cadillac was too big to get into most spaces along the street, and even when a vacant spot was available he didn't have the dexterity to get into it. He cursed some drivers in English, others in Italian and waved a big plump finger at the rest. It was a four-block walk from Sorento's employee parking lot to the restaurant. Although it was November it was still warm. Sweat beaded up on Swag's forehead, his breath was heavy and his short arms were moving mechanically around his plump belly. Swag looked as much like Peter Clemenza, the murderous character in The Godfather, that he often theorized that Mario Puzo modeled Clemenza after him.

Swag was out of breath when he entered the restaurant. The waiters and waitress greeted him warmly – like an uncle who was dropping in for a visit. In the kitchen a young man in a tomato sauce covered apron waved, "Hey, Bobby. What's up." Swag raised a hand and kept walking. Two others smiled and spoke. Swag stopped for an instant and popped a meatball into his mouth. "The best job I ever had was workin' in a kitchen. That's how I got this," he smacked his stomach creating a sound like plunking a watermelon. The boys in the kitchen laughed.

Swag walked through a hallway and knocked twice. "Come in, you half-kraut moron," Carlos Triano shouted. Swag walked quickly inside and shut the door. "I told you to get money outta Sweeney. I didn't say blow his brains out!"

"I know what you said, but that loser wasn't ever gonna come up with no money."

"You don't kill anybody without me say'n to kill 'em," Triano growled.

"Boss, I ain't never gonna be no "made man," but my Ma was born right down there in Hell's Kitchen, and I'm as much Corgliano as I am Swag, and it ain't right that guys like me can never get all the way in. It ain't right for you to call me half-kraut, and piss on my accomplishments. I'm a good soldier, Boss, and I know how to make decisions. That Arthur Sweeney wouldn't ever gonna come up with no money!"

"Sit down, Bobby, before you have a heart attack." Triano said.

"Boss, I been the muscle for this part of the family for twenty years, I know when to pop the cork on somebody."

Sweat ran down Swag's forehead and settled into his eyebrow. Triano's expression had changed from anger to one as mellow as a grandfather watching his toddler grandson. "It's okay, Bobby, settle down."

Swag was calmer as he sat back in his chair, his breathing returned to normal. He opened the plastic folder he carried in and took out the sheet of paper from Sweeney's home. He slid it across Triano's desk.

"What is this, Bobby?" Triano's brow furrowed as he picked it up.

"You ever heard of John Mccan?" Swag asked.

"No. I don't know any John Mccan."

"John Mccan wrote a song called American Pie back in the sixties on a piece of paper and he auctioned it off not too long ago for four and a half million dollars." Swag said, trying to recall exactly what Sweeney had told him.

"This don't say nothin' about no John Mccan, or American Pie. It says *Another Stain on The Old Banner."* Triano said.

"John Mccan didn't write this. Sweeney said. John Wilkes Booth wrote this. Sweeney said it was worth a hundred times what the American Pie was worth." Swag said.

Triano got up from his chair and walked around his desk and then to the door. There was a man standing in the hallway; a double barrel shotgun propped against the wall. "Get Vinney," he said.

In a moment the young man who had spoken to Swag when he entered was standing there, wiping his hands on his apron. "What's up?"

"Bobby says John Mccan sold a song about American pie for four and a half million dollars"

"It's not about John Mccan, Boss. It's about that paper," Swag interrupted. He was getting hot under the collar again. Swag and Triano had been together for thirty years, and heated arguments between them were not uncommon. Triano tolerated more from Swag than he would have any other grunt in the organization.

"I need to know if what he was saying was true, Bobby." Triano said.

"It don't matter about the American Pie. It's the John Wilkes Booth paper!" Swag said again.

Vinney laughed. "It wasn't John Mccan. It was a Don Mclean's song. He sold the rough draft for millions. It was big news on the web. Some collector bought it on auction."

"What's this?" Triano asked, handing the paper to Vinney. He looked at it and then read it out loud. "*Another stain on the old banner-jwb.*" He paused and then read it out loud again. "I don't know what it is," he said, shrugging his shoulders.

"Get on your computer and find out," Triano said. Vinney looked at Triano, his eyes transmitted a huge signal of doubt. "People know what goes on on the computer, Boss."

"This ain't nothing the Feds would have an interest in, Vinney. Just do as I say."

After a few moments Vinney was back with the information on Booth and how he had shouted, " *Another stain on the old banner*," before he was shot by Boston Corbert. At that point the conversation became more detailed. Swag related what Sweeney told him about the other seventeen missing pages from Booth's diary, and finally that Bradley Sweeney and Owen Black were in possession of them. Carlos Triano wasn't convinced that a piece of paper was worth anything unless it was plated in gold, but he agreed to let Swag work on it. He assigned Swag to take one man and find Owen and Bradley and get the other seventeen pages of Booth's diary.

As Swag left the office Triano said, "Oh, Bobby, don't kill anybody unless I say so, alright?"

"I won't, Boss. I don't like it down here. I sure don't want to come back explaining myself again. They got them maître D's standing out on the sidewalk with a white towel on their arms trying to bully people into going inside like them barkers at a carnival, and down in China Town ,they ain't even all Chinks anymore. They got Mungs, and Koreans and all kinds a gooks down there trying to get you into an alley to buy a phony Rolex. It's like a God-damned circus here in Manhatton.

"Bobby! Don't kill anybody unless I say so! Got it?" Triano said firmly.

"I got it, Boss. Don't kill nobody unless you say so."

Chapter Twelve

Arthur Sweeney spent several days rotting in his home before a representative of the homeowners' association came back to follow up on the condition of his property. He didn't like the horrific stench emanating from the house so he called 911. Upon arrival the police suspected a decaying corpse. They had to break the door down to gain entry. It was stifling inside Sweeney's home so the guys in the hazmat suits were called in to assist with the crime scene.

Swag had been conducting business for so long that he knew how to do the job without leaving evidence behind. Sooner or later Arthur Sweeney's murder would be an unsolved murder mystery. Still there was something interesting that Sweeney left behind. Charlottesville detectives checked the activity on his computer and his cell phone for clues. There was an unusual amount of views regarding the phrase, *Another stain on the old banner.* He had also downloaded examples of John Wilkes Booth's handwriting. Those things would not have been suspicious activity for someone in Sweeney's occupation, but a backup was made and logged into evidence along with a mountain of other things from the scene.

Bradley had Arthur's body cremated and he and Owen picked up his ashes at the crematory. When they left the parking lot, Arthur's ashes sat behind the truck seat with

Edwin Stanton's satchel, resting in eternal peace. At that point Booth's diary wasn't much of a concern. They returned to work gutting the building. Bradley accepted that Arthur was murdered because of his gambling debts, and he wasn't wrong.

Sometimes people are excited about unlikely possibilities, like winning the lottery, or landing the perfect job, and they talk about what they're going to do with all that money when it comes rolling in, but time passes wiping away whimsical thoughts, and they settle back into reality . That was the case with Booth's diary. Owen and Bradley didn't have any evidence that it was or it wasn't Booth's , but as the days passed the excitement was dwindling. Now it was just sitting there unsecured in the truck. Both Owen and Bradley wanted to follow up on finding the page they left with Arthur, but all that plaster and wall debris had taken precedence. Working for a living was Owen's reality.

That wasn't the case for Robert Swag. His interest was growing as information came in about the value of Abraham Lincoln artifacts. Since Swag didn't have a lot of interest in technology other than listening devices and alarm systems, he was relying on the organization to provide whatever information he needed to determine the diary's value and authenticity. Still he wanted the entire kit and kaboodle before getting too deep into the weeds. He knew there were auction sites on what Sweeney had called "the dark web," but that wasn't his concern. The boss said to get the diary and that was what he was going to do. Whatever cash came out of this deal belonged to the family.

Still behind the scenes people were searching the internet and making telephone calls all over Washington, believing that the FBI wouldn't find anything strange about that. Carlos Triano was the gambling syndicate head honcho, but he wasn't without accountability. He had bosses too. There was prostitution, protection, bribery, and all manner of criminal enterprises within the organization and each division had a boss. Triano didn't have free reign to do as he pleased. Although killing Sweeney wasn't all that consequential , it still had to be explained. The best way was to show a little profit. He didn't believe Booth's diary was worth millions but he knew there would be some fool somewhere who would dole out a hundred grand even if it turned out to be nothing more than a bunch of time-yellowed paper. The problem was that the searches Triano's people were making were leaving a trail – a trail the FBI were reviewing because the mob was always on their radar; anything they did was worth looking at. Another factor was that Arthur Sweeney had also been a person of interest because of his gambling and contacts with certain underworld characters. Arthur's recent searches and inquiries on the web matched those of the mob, and Arthur mysteriously had the back of his head blown off.

Things at the FBI were changing too. Lee Ford stopped in front of the FBI Bureau office on Fourth Street in Washington D.C. He waited as the tall black man dressed in a charcoal suit approached his car. Lee was agitated. Any veteran agent in his situation would be. His distinguished career had lasted eighteen years, and now he was lowered to breaking in a rookie agent fresh from Quantico, Virginia. It was an assignment designed to humiliate him. As the young agent slipped into the passenger seat he stuck out his hand, "I'm Tyrese Jefferson." Lee looked straight ahead, "Lee Ford," he grunted.

Tyrese laughed.

"What's so funny?" Lee asked curtly.

"Well – you sort of snorted your name. I thought it was funny."

"I never snorted, and I don't see anything funny about it."

"Maybe we should start over, Agent Ford. I'm Tyrese Jefferson. I've been assigned to work with you for a few weeks. I'm pleased to meet you," Tyrese said. Lee didn't answer. He put the car into gear drove to Pennsylvania Avenue and headed west. After twenty minutes Lee finally spoke. "The Bureau is screwing with me. We don't have a thing to do. They put you with me just to emphasize how little power I have left."

"Why? What's the problem?" Tyrese asked.

"It's a long story, but it boils down to the fact that I was in charge of a team and we lost our guy and he turned up in Russia."

"What was up with this guy? What did he do?"

"It was something like Edward Snowden," Lee said.

"You lost Edward Snowden. Wow!" Tyrese gasped.

"No! It wasn't Edward Snowden! I said something like Edward Snowden," Lee snapped. He looked straight ahead again.

"So. Now we're just going to drive around all day?" Tyrese said.

"Yes, we're just going to drive around – anyway until 10 o'clock," Lee said. "The Chief is in a meeting so I'm supposed to keep you entertained until then. I guess he'll give us a case, but I don't know for sure. Whatever it is, it won't amount to anything."

Tyrese didn't answer.

"You drew a shitty hand when they stuck you with me," Lee said apologetically.

At 10 they were waiting in John Wodetzki's office. When he entered Tyrese was quick to rise. Wodetzki went immediately to Tyrese extending a hand. "Welcome aboard," he said. He glanced at Lee without saying anything. It was a tempestuous glance with the corners of his mouth slightly turning up. He pitched a leather folder across his desk and then took a seat. "I've got a case for you, Lee," he said.

"I'm ready for whatever it is, John," Lee said apathetically.

Wodetzki opened the folder, scanned through the pages, raised his eyes and stated, "You know what happens when you lose someone like Snowden, don't you, Lee?"

Tyrese's eyes widen. "It was Snowden!" he gasped.

"I said it was something like Snowden," Wodetzki said.

"What is it, John. Let's not mess around." Lee said.

"When you lose someone like that you get cases like the Rosewell alien crash, or the Kennedy conspiracy fifty years after it was settled or Clinton's Marcy Park investigation." Lee rolled his eyes. Tyrese was puzzled. It was obvious that Lee and Wodetzki were well acquainted, and probably friends, but there was an undercurrent that he didn't quite get.

Wodetzki went on to explain that there had been chatter and rumors floating around about John Wilkes Booth's diary. "Believe it or not the mob is interested in it for some reason," Wodetzki laughed.

Lee sighed. "John, I read the internet. I know Edwin Stanton murdered President Lincoln and Boston Corbet murdered Booth to keep him from talking. Case solved!" Lee stated facetiously.

"Just one problem, some loser who was into the mob for a hundred grand took a .38 caliber in the back of his head, and they were all onto the same page when it came to the John Wilkes Booth's missing diary. Sweeney and the mob both repeatedly searched a phrase Booth shouted before being shot."

"Strange," Tyrese said.

Wodetzki slid the folder across the desk and said, "Take Trace here and check it out,"

The young agent stuck out his hand to shake, "That's Tyrese, Chief."

"That's what I said, Tyrese. Good luck."

Chapter Thirteen

Carlos Triano sent Ricardo Costa to assist Robert Swag in locating Owen Black and Bradley Sweeney. He gave Costa the same warning he gave Swag. "Don't kill anybody." Ricardo was a young Italian upstart who talked the talk but he had never been tested. Still that didn't keep him from boasting about putting a cap into anybody who crossed his path. He wanted people to believe he was a bloodthirsty sonofabitch. Whether he was or not was yet to be seen.

Swag met Costa in a bar in Jersey City across the bay from New York City. It was dark inside, the oil floors and checkered tablecloths were reminiscent of the thirties and forties, a humongous mirror hung behind the bar, the walls lined with partially filled liquor bottles. Four men occupied stools at the bar, all of them connected with organized crime. Three of them were in their twenties and the fourth in his sixties. Costa was sitting at a table in a corner in the back. When Swag entered the four men all spoke, calling him Bobby. Swag waved before going into a tirade. "I almost got taken out by a frickin' train. Where else in the country they got trains driving down the middle of the street besides Jersey!"

"Trains come down the street in Jersey City, Bobby. You gotta get used to it," the older guy said.

"It ain't right," Swag said.

While walking back to Costa's table one of the young mobsters said, "You got something big going down, Bobby?" The other three laughed. Swag's eyes narrowed and his lips tightened. "It's need to know only," Swag growled.

"I heard you capped some loser for some worthless papers." More laughter. Swag walked on scowling. When he sat down at Costa's table he grunted as his rotund frame settled into the chair. "So, you're the hotshot they sent me to do this job?" Swag asked. "Yeah, chasing some kinda stupid shit," Costa said. "I ain't lookin' for no crap from you, asshole. You do what I tell ya," Swag snarled, still irritated by being laughed at.

Costa smiled, "Swag, I'm all Italian and I'll be a made man someday and you'll be taking orders from me."

"Right now you're doin' what I say to do." Swag said. He thought for a moment and then said, "Did you ever see that movie *Goodfellas* when they told Tommy Divito he was a made man. Right after that they took him out into a corn field and beat him like a dog and then buried him alive. Sometimes that's what happens to smartasses like you. And another thing, people call me Bobby, or Mr. Swag. You don't call me Swag, got it!"

"Bobby, *Goodfellas*, that was a movie, wasn't it."

"So was the *Godfather* – tell me that shit wasn't true." Swag smirked.

When they left Jersey City Swag was feeling a little foolish. What if this John Wilkes Booth diary was total folly? He didn't like Costa and he knew Costa would try to humiliate him if this turned into a cluster-fuck. That was the kind of brash upstarts they had in the organization these days. Costa just didn't know who he was messing with though. Swag was a very dangerous man, and he was Carlos Triano's right-hand man.

They drove Swag's Cadillac from Jersey to Washington D.C without talking most of the way. It was as hard for Swag as it was for Costa. It was Bobby's nature to pitch a fit at other drivers and go into tirades about how stupid some of them were. He needed to verbalize everything he was thinking so the three and a half-hour drive was excruciating. It was just as bad for Costa. The layers of fat covering Bobby's body insulated him from the cold. Sometimes even in the 30-degree weather, beads of sweat formed on his upper lip. The heater was off the entire way. Costa was reed thin, olive tinted skin, and his black hair slicked back giving him that Italiano look. He had a two-day beard, unshaven by design, and his teeth were clenched to keep them from chattering. By the time they reached Baltimore Costa was as tense as a man awaiting execution. His internal oblique muscles were so tight that he couldn't move without shaking. Finally, he couldn't take it anymore. "Bobby, how about some heat." The tone of his voice conciliatory.

Swag liked it that Costa voice was different now. To him it said, "alright, I know you're the boss." He smiled and slid the lever to the red mark. "I'll warm you up then I gotta turn it back down. I can't take all that heat."

"I got Icicles hanging outta my nose, Bobby" Costa laughed.

Swag laughed too, and then he began cursing every driver that came down the pike. Now he was completely unfettered. By the time they arrived in D.C. they were as jovial as two comedians reliving every criminal act they had ever committed for the organization. Costa had to fabricate a few escapades validating his manhood, but Swag knew it and let it go. Costa even called Swag, Boss, a couple of times causing the big cat to smile from ear to ear. Now it seemed like finding Owen and Bradley would be a piece of cake.

It was already getting dark at 5:00 p.m., as Swag drove down Edmondson Street. Soft burnish light filtered onto the brick pavers, women in big ticket dresses pranced into and out of shops with shopping bags in hand. Santa Claus rung the Salvation Army Bell on the corner. Bobby made several illegal u-turns looking for a parking spot on the street before finally finding a customer lot in the alley.

Inside Warburton's Bar and Grill people from government offices and international corporations were gathering getting drunk, complaining about their co-workers and talking shop. It was Friday and the regulars laid low because it was a different crowd. They were all dressed in designer clothes and expensive footwear. In contrast Swag looked like a brown bear wrapped in a rusty three-piece suit he might have bargained for at the Goodwill Store in Newark. Costa had on a black button-down shirt, a thin gray tie, and a black knee length trench coat. One young woman snickered after they passed her. She could not have known that Swag could come up with more cash than the entire house, although ill-gotten.

Costa followed as Swag made his way to the back of the bar. Costa showed little patience as he was squeezed by unknown patrons standing between the bar and their tables. He gave one sleekly dressed young man a straight arm as he pressed through, garnering a stern glance. When the kid's eyes met Costa's glare he wilted immediately. All tables were occupied, but in the farthest corner there was one guy sitting at a table with four empty chairs. Swag walked up and stood over him. He was wearing designer jeans and a t-shirt that said GYM RAT, the same guy who had the altercation with Owen Black. He had his boot resting on one of the chairs. Swag raised his leg, grunted, and kicked Gym Rat's foot with a thud. Shocked, he scrambled to regain his balance. He glared at Swag with intensity. Swag said, "Move it, you fuck'n faggot!"

Gym rat sputtered, "These chairs are for my buddies."

"I don't give a fuck, move it!"

Costa stood behind Swag staring down at Gym Rat. Fear was plastered on his face as he pushed his chair back and wandered into the crowd. Now that there was an empty table Swag and Costa sat down. Swag lit up a cigar right beneath the no smoking sign. Chloe, the waitress, was quick to respond. "You can't smoke in here," she said. Swag turned the cigar in his cheek.

The bartender, a fifties something Irishman with broad shoulders and a head full of graying hair walked up behind her. "I'm Sean Ryan, I'm the bartender and co-owner here. It's a rule here that you can't smoke, and there's no smoking laws. You have to put that out." He said, pointing a calloused finger at Swag's cigar. Swag nonchalantly held the cigar up for Ryan to take it. Ryan looked at it for a moment, relieved Swag of the cigar and dropped it into the glass Gym Rat had left behind.

"What can I get you, boys?" Ryan asked, studying them intently.

"We ain't really wanting nothin' to drink or eat, but we are looking for a couple a your customers." Swag said.

"This isn't the post office, but just for curiosity sake, who might that be?"

"You got an Owen Black and a Bradley Sweeney?"

"They got some kind of debt to pay?" Ryan asked.

"Why would you ask that?" Costa said.

Sean studied Swag's face ignoring Costa. "I used to tend bar up there in Manhatton. I was down at Rock'n Riley's for awhile, and in the Empire State building at the State Grill and Bar. I even did a stint at the Café Wha when I was young and I worked the bars over there on E Street in Jersey.

"What's that gotta do with Owen Black and Bradley Sweeney?" Swag said.

"It's just my way of saying I've been around. I know when there's muscle in the place. What's the mob want with my customers anyway?"

"We ain't no mob," Costa said.

"Yeah, and I ain't no bartender," Ryan said. He pointed to the surveillance cameras in the ceiling and over the doors." I'm betting the FBI will want these video tapes if anything happens to me, or to Owen and Bradley."

Swag scooted his chair away from the table and headed for the door. Costa followed. When they were on the sidewalk Costa said, "Bobby, lets cap that fuck'n mick!"

"The boss said don't kill nobody. Besides Ricky, we can't go around killin' everybody who gives us some shit." Swag said. Oddly, Swag was the voice of reason.

"Whatta we gonna do now, Bobby?"

"Did ya see that girl? She was listening to everything we said. She knows them guys. If I know women, she'll light out as soon as she gets a chance to tell 'em we're lookin' for 'em." Swag said.

"You know women, huh Bobby?" Costa asked with a smile.

"Yeah, I know women," Swag said.

"You got sisters?" Costa laughed, hitting Swag across the shoulder.

Swag chuckled.

They waited on the bench across from Santa Claus. It was two hours before Chloe came out the front door and headed for the alley to access the parking lot. Costa commented on how convenient it was that she was parked in the same parking lot they were in. She didn't notice them following her as she hurried to her 2002 Toyota.

Just as Swag had predicted Chloe drove straight to the narrow three-story brick building where Owen and Bradley were staying. A light snow was falling but the moon was shining through the clouds. A midnight blue sky above let the twinkling stars shine vaguely through the snowflakes, as lights from the city and those of the apartment buildings and condos created a translucent vanilla glow at rooftop level. It was strangely beautiful, so much so that it didn't escape the notice of Bobby Swag. He wiped the inside windshield with a towel he had stuffed into the side pocket of his door panel. "This is beautiful, this snow and them lights. It's like a picture in one of them little kid books about Sanny Claus." Costa agreed.

"We gonna go in, or wait until they come out?" Costa asked.

"Probably best to wait until the girl's gone. We don't need no more to deal with than we hafta," Swag said. "That's too bad. I wouldn't mind going a round or two with that girl," Costa hummed.

She wouldn't be interested in either of us, Ricky." Swag said.

Chloe was tall, her skin tan and smooth, thick brown shoulder length hair and her deep brown inquisitive eyes were stunning. Men at the bar hit on her so frequently that she didn't even think about it anymore. Having anything to do with either of them would have been digging deeper than the bottom of the barrel.

"It don't matter if she's interested or not, if you know what I mean," Costa said.

Swags eyes narrowed, his brow furrowed. "Listen, Ricky. We ain't messing with no girl. We ain't forcin' no girl to do nothing against her will. We ain't raping no girl or nothing like that! We're gonna get them papers and that's it!"

"You're the boss, Bobby, I'm just sayin'." Costa said shrugging his shoulders.

Chloe was inside for forty-five minutes before she came down and left in her car. The sky had darkened, the snow gone, fog was beginning to form creating a gray cloud at street level. The only lights on in the building were on the third level, Owen and Bradley's place. Swag got out of the car and popped the trunk open to retrieve a double barrel sawed-off shotgun. A frigid breeze stirred the Bradford Pear trees along the sidewalk, sending a ribbon-like band of fog down the street. When Swag and Costa walked into the mist, the dim glow from the streetlights projected eerie ghostly silhouettes behind them.

Chloe's visit left Owen and Bradley guessing as to why two suspicious looking characters would be asking questions about them. Bradley was first to suggest that maybe it had something to do with his father. He didn't have any doubts that Arthur was murdered over his gambling debts. Yet he didn't know how that would involve him. Owen didn't disagree. It never crossed either of their minds that the paper in the satchel behind the seat of the F150 had left a target on both of their backs.

Bradley sat on his bed resting his chin in his hand. Owen walked to the window. The lighted dome on the Capitol was a blur in the distance. He looked down and saw two figures moving rapidly towards their front door. When Swag passed under the light Owen saw the shotgun.

"Bradley, get up!"

Bradley's eyes widened, startled he bolted upright. "What is it?"

"We got problems," Owen said.

"What is it?" Bradley asked again.

"We've got company and it doesn't look good. There's two guys at the stairs and one of them has a shotgun." Owen said, trying to stay calm. Back in the day this would be the time to lock and load, but Owen didn't have a weapon, not even a knife.

As Swag and Costa stepped inside the stairwell Costa said, "I thought Mr. Triano said not to kill anybody."

"We ain't gonna kill nobody. This double barrel shorty will put the fear a God in 'em. They just need to give us them papers and we'll be back in Jersey before morning."

"How about this?" Costa asked, revealing his 9 millimeter.

"Just leave that in your pants. I'll do the talkin'."

Owen quickly assessed his options, knowing they were trapped if they remained in the room. It was so small there wasn't a defensive position anywhere. "Bradley, I have to get outside this room. There's a small alcove outside the bathroom. I'll get out there and wait. You stay here, I won't let them get inside."

The stairs creaked as Swag led the way, huffing for air before he got to the second level. When they were halfway up the final leg Swag stopped to catch his breath. Costa laughed, placed a hand on Swag's broad back and gave him a push. When they topped the third level Swag stopped again for a moment, broke down the shotgun and shoved two twelve-gauge shells into the dual chambers.

Owen was glued to the wall in the shadows. His heart was racing, his right hand was shaking violently. He closed his hand, squeezing tightly to slow it down. With his teeth clenched, he waited.

The light beneath the door illuminated the floor in the hallway as long shadows were cast onto the walls. Swag knocked but there was no answer. Owen held his breath. He was only a few feet away from fighting his way out or disaster.

Swag knocked again. Bradley answered, "Who is it?"

"You're Uncle Charley, open the frickin door." Swag demanded. Bradley didn't answer. "Kick it," Swag said, giving Costa a head nod. Costa kicked and the heavy thud echoed down the hallway. The sturdy wooden door did not break. He kicked again and the lower panel cracked. Swag lunged into the door with his thick shoulder. The hinges popped, the door slammed sideways and dropped to the floor. Swag shoved the barrel of the shotgun through the doorway.

Owen came out of the shadows close to the floor like a cat moving quickly. He hit Costa from behind sending him skidding across the floor. Swag turned, startled, his eyes were wide open as he tried to find the source of the onrush. A deafening roar from the gun barrel rung out as the buckshot ripped into the ceiling, as Swag pulled the trigger. Owen grabbed the shotgun, twisted it against Swag's thumbs dislodging it from his grasp. Costa was up advancing towards Owen with an extended arm and a nine-millimeter in his fist. Owen cracked the twelve-gauge barrel across Costa's head sending him back to the floor. Swag grabbed Owen from behind, snorting ,"You motherfucker!"

Bradley rushed out of the room with his computer in hand. With both hands he smashed it across Swags head. Swag went down to his knees. Owen pressed the gun barrels against Swag's head. "Don't move," he shouted.

"Do you know who you're fuckin' with, motherfucker." Swag growled.

"Is there anybody else after us? Others here with you?" Owen asked, cocking the hammer back on the shotgun. Swag glared at Owen but he didn't answer.

Costa was moving again. Owen ordered Bradley to get down the stairs. He drew back the gun butt and slammed it hard into Swag's forehead and then he hit Costa with a three-sixty swing of the shotgun bashing his left arm. Both he and Bradley scrambled down the steps and out into the parking lot behind the building.

"Get that cell phone out and call 911," Owen said excitedly.

"It's in the room," Bradley said.

"There may be others. We need to find a defensive position somewhere in the alley," Owen said as he led the way towards a narrow passageway between the buildings. They found a rusty metal fire escape, hurried up to the second level and waited. Owen checked the shotgun to find one spent shell and one unspent in the chamber.

Swag and Costa limped out the front door and crossed the street to Swag's Cadillac. Costa carried the nine-millimeter in his right hand, his other arm hung limply to his side, apparently broken. As they turned onto Seventeenth Street there was an oscillating blur of red and blue light shining through the foggy mist.

"What a cluster-fuck! What in the fuck happened back there!" Costa shouted.

"I don't know," muttered Swag. "It ain't good."

With that said they were on their way back to New Jersey.

It wasn't over for the other two. When three Washington, D.C. squad cars rolled to a stop, six uniformed officers advanced upon the building with shotguns at ready. One by one they filed into the stairwell, and then upstairs. Two partially dressed occupants were waiting, excitedly relating the melee to the police.

When Owen and Bradley made their way out of the alley, Owen held the shotgun over his head in open view. The officers were loud, ordering them onto their knees with their hands locked behind their heads, and then outstretched onto their stomachs. They were both handcuffed, picked up and shoved chest first against a brick wall. With an officer on each arm, their legs were separated, shoved backward leaving them leaning at a thirty-degree angle. Any movement from that position would cause them to fall face first onto the ground. They were questioned aggressively for several minutes before it was determined they were the intended victims.

The police took the shotgun into evidence, called a crime scene crew, transported Owen and Bradley to the precinct and filed their reports. They were both astounded by what had happened, and Bradley offered that maybe it had something to do with his deceased father having heavy gambling losses. After being released they returned to their room. The landlord was there hanging a blue tarp over the broken doorway. He was outraged about the incident. He insinuated they were into drugs and crime, but after questioning them he realized they were just as puzzled about what had happened as he was.

The towel Swag had used to wipe the windshield of his car was now pressed against his head as deep red blotches were soaking through. Costa's arm was broken and both eyes were swollen nearly shut and encircled by deepening dark bruises. His right eyebrow had been laid open and was now crusted with dry blood.

Costa's mind was churning. He wanted to know the identity of the man who had injured him. Killing him would be a pleasure. He would torture him. He would beat him senseless, like Tommy Divito in *Goodfellas*, and then bury him alive. Costa's jaw was clenched in hate. All he could think about was revenge.

Swag was thinking about how the wise guys in the bar had laughed at him. This thing with the Booth diary was beginning to look like a total mess – a disaster! He didn't intend to go back to Carlos Triano empty-handed with his head knocked open and his partner dragging a broken arm. This frickin thing had to be settled.

Chapter Fourteen

Owen and Bradley were on edge as they went back to work. Both of them were on guard for suspicious movements or noises inside the building or outside. It was exhausting. Although neither were hungry they finished for the evening and stopped at Warburton's for a sandwich and beer. When they entered Chloe hurried to Bradley and threw her arms around him. "Thank God you're alright!" she said. Bradley blushed, but he was obviously grateful. She held on to his elbow and walked with him to the rear portion of the bar. It was easy to see Chloe was head over heels. Owen and Bradley sat down and Chloe joined them. Chloe signaled for another waitress to take their order. She watched Bradley with adoring eyes as he explained in detail how the attack had gone down. Owen thankfully emphasized how important it was that she had warned them. "Otherwise, we'd probably be toast right now," he said.

Sean Ryan stepped out of his office and saw them sitting there. He stopped at the end of the bar and gave them a head nod. "We need to talk," he said, walking towards his office door. They raised their eyebrows, looked inquisitively at each other as they followed. Once inside Sean sat on his desk and crossed his arms. "Boys, I think you're in trouble."

"You think," Owen said incredulously.

"I mean, big trouble. Trouble that won't go away," Sean said.

"I think it's all about Arthur, and now about me. If I go back to Charlottesville Owen will be out of this," Bradley said quietly.

"That's not going to happen," Owen said.

Rumors in the neighborhood were that Owen had pretty much annihilated both attackers. Sean was solemn when he spoke about this very serious situation, but behind a concerned face he wanted to smile when he thought about Bradley hitting one of the guys in the head with a computer. He was strong and fit, but he had never had to defend himself in his life.

"I know these guys, Owen, they want something from you and you don't stand a chance with them. They're going to get it, or they'll get even with you for not having it. These are connected people and now they have a grudge to settle."

"What are you suggesting, Sean?" Owen asked.

"I know you know how to defend yourself, but I think you have to get out of here. Go back to Kentucky, or out west. Just don't stick around here." Sean said.

Owen watched Sean intently. "Won't they try to find us wherever we go?"

"I don't know, but you're not safe here. You're welcome here in the bar anytime. I want you to know that, but I'll worry."

Owen spent so many years fighting, killing people and breaking things, that he should have been habituated to it, but he wasn't. He didn't want to spend his nights sleeping on edge, his eyes trained to flash open at sounds in the night, or to forget how to laugh out loud again. He'd been carefree here. He knew his future wasn't going to be so bright, but he was resigned to working for a living and making the best of it. Now, what would happen? Would he stay and fight or move on? He knew one thing, whatever he decided to do it included Bradley. Although they didn't know who, or why they were targets, it was certain they had a common enemy.

At FBI headquarters Lee Ford was reviewing the search records of Arthur Sweeney when Tyrese Jefferson came into his office. "There's something we need to check out," Tyrese said.

"Okay. What have you got?" Lee said, moving away from his computer.

"The locals got a call - shots fired at a rooming house in the fourth precinct. When they got there everything was over with, but from everything they could determine a couple of hoods broke into an apartment and tried to kill some guys who live there."

"What happened? What's that got to do with us?" Lee asked.

"One of them was Arthur Sweeney's son."

"Huh, interesting."

"The other guy is Owen Black." Tyrese said, his brow furrowed.

"Anything on him."

"War hero – Silver Star medal. He's been in some real bad stuff according to the Chief of Police in his hometown. The Navy recruiter said he tried to re-enlist, but they're not taking guys like him these days. Too damaged."

"How did this guy do in the attack?"

"I guess he kicked ass." Tyrese smiled slightly.

"They don't want guys who can kick ass in the military anymore? It's a new world, man," Lee chuckled.

After making a few preliminary calls Lee and Tyrese received e-mails from the precinct with details. They didn't have anything on either Owen or Bradley other than what they had learned on the reports from the patrol division. They were both clean. The other information about them came from follow-up Tyrese had done. With that information under their hats they were off to the neighborhood to dig up what they could find. Although Lee still scoffed at a John Wilkes Booth conspiracy theory, the fact that Arthur Sweeney had been murdered, and now his son was involved in something pretty questionable, piqued his interest.

Owen and Bradley were gone when Lee and Tyrese got to their apartment. There was a blue tarp across the door, the room was empty, and neighbors could only report that the two men who lived there packed up a military duffle bag, a small suitcase and left in a red Ford 150. One of the neighbors said that they hung around at Warburton's Bar and Grill.

When Lee and Tyrese got to Warburton's Sean Ryan was standing behind the bar drinking coffee. The place was empty except for two waitresses at a table wiping glasses with a towel. Sean watched them suspiciously. He knew a detective when he saw one, but they were a little more frayed around the edges than these guys. His guess was they were the Feds. "What's up, gentlemen."

"We're doing a little follow-up on an incident from a couple of days ago," Lee said flipping his badge. "A couple of your regulars were attacked in their apartment over on Edmundson Street. We thought maybe there was a little more info still out here the cops haven't dug up."

"So the FBI is investigating local crime now," Sean said.

"We're interested. It's something that might relate to what we've got going on. Just a few questions," Tyrese said.

Sean related what he had heard from rumors, leaving out what he had learned from Owen and Bradley firsthand. Sean was a little critical of the local cops that they hadn't interviewed him because he had something that he thought would be helpful. The two wise guys who were there looking for Owen and Bradley would have been at the top of the suspect list, but nobody asked. They went to the office where Sean keyed up the video on his computer showing video of Swag and Costa.

"These two guys were in here, smoking, giving my customers a hard time, showing their asses, and asking questions about Owen and Bradley. I know it had to be these guys who tried to kill them. They were mob guys. It was easy to see," Sean said.

"Do you think Owen and Bradley are into something?" Lee asked.

"No, these guys are clean. Bradley is a kid. He's as innocent as a newborn baby. One of my waitresses has it bad for him, but he's so shy he can't even make a move. Owen's just a good guy. These guys are clean. They're as puzzled by what happened as the cops are."

When Lee saw Swag and Costa on the screen he immediately recognized Swag. "That's Bobby Swag. He's the muscle for Carlos Triano out of Jersey. He's a real menace. If we ever get the goods on him we'll be digging up bodies all over the country."

"I'm worried about those two boys. I advised them to get out of here. I haven't seen them since. Maybe they took my advice," Sean said.

"Maybe," Lee said. He gave Sean his card and asked him to call if anything came up.

Chapter Fifteen

The mist floated lazily across the mountain tops, capped by a golden haze, blending into the clouds as the sun dipped below the horizon. Owen took it all in as he navigated the narrow blacktop road that had been transformed into a brilliant sienna ribbon weaving into the dark shadows of twilight. He had joined the Navy to see the world, but now as he journeyed through corridors and passageways of northern Georgia he was astounded by its beauty and regretted not seeing more of the U.S. in his thirty-nine years on earth instead of heading off into Afghanistan.

Bradley was sleeping, his head pressed against the window, as much at ease as though the last few weeks had never happened. Owen's young friend was a quiet soul and seemed well-adjusted despite being raised in a place where love was in short supply. He was sturdy and calm in the face of adversity, and even danger. Now in the aftermath of dodging an attempt on his life it seemed like just another day at the office. When Owen told him that they had to leave D.C., he just said, "Okay."

Owen examined his own perspective and realized it was the same for him. Although they were moving on it wasn't like there was an extreme urgency to get somewhere. Avoiding a situation was a more appropriate terminology. He had experienced many situations more hair-raising than what had happened in their apartment, but back then he didn't have the choice to move on.

Now he did.

Arthur Sweeney's ashes were still behind the seat snugly pressed up against the ancient leather satchel with Edwin Stanton's name stamped into the flap. Owen thought about what might be contained within those pages; the information according to Bradley might change history. He liked Bradley a lot, but he was a strange duck. "Okay, he thought, whatever there is in that satchel has been there for a hundred and fifty years. It will change nothing to leave it, or to expose it to scrutiny, but it might change Bradley. So just leave it alone for now." It had certainly lost its importance.

Blackness descended upon the hills as the sun disappeared beyond the horizon. There wasn't a light anywhere except for billions of stars twinkling in the sky. Bradley was awake, simply watching the road disappear beneath the wheels of the 150, content just to ride along in the passenger seat.

"Do you know where we are, Brad?" Owen asked.

"No, I don't," he answered.

"I think we're somewhere in Georgia." Owen said.

"Not sure though?" Bradley asked.

"Not sure at all."

Just then they topped a hill where dim lights of a roadside tavern were visible ahead. A neon sign with several missing letters advertised cold beer and sandwiches. Owen rolled into the gravel parking lot weaving to miss huge water-filled potholes, and horse manure. There were as many hitching-post as parking spaces, but only one old mare was hitched, stretching her neck over the pole to nibble on the weeds growing beneath it.

"Looks like a growing concern," Owen chuckled as they entered. It was dreary inside with a combination of early seventies chairs and formica tabletops, dry clumps of mud and most likely other material from the parking lot were visible on the floor. Having a sandwich was completely out of the question, but a cold beer was in order.

Owen inspected the chairs before taking a seat but even as he did, he wasn't convinced he would find a clean one in the dimly lighted bar. Bradley didn't seem to be concerned. A sixties age woman wearing a grease-covered apron approached with a cigarette dangling from her lips and a pad and pen in hand.

"Help ya?" She asked.

Owen ordered two draft beers.

"Okay, but I gotta see some id from the boy," she said, nodding towards Bradley. She waited with one hand turned outward with the fold of her wrist resting on her hip. Bradley opened his wallet and handed her his Virginia driver's license. "You look different than this," she said.

"I've lost some weight," Bradley said.

"Ya sure have. You was kinda chubby weren't ya."

Bradley smiled, but he didn't answer.

After returning with the beer the woman said, "Well, anyways, happy birthday,"

Owens brow furrowed, a slight grin brightened his face. "This is your birthday? How old are you?" he asked.

"Yup, this is my birthday. I'm twenty-two."

"Huh, what do you know about that! You should have said something. I could have bought you a cupcake with a candle on it or something. We could have had a little fun."

"What could be more fun than riding all over Georgia with your best friend and your dad and having a beer in a place like this."

"Where's your dad?" the waitress asked.

"He's in the truck," Bradley said. The waitress stretched her neck trying to look out the window. Owen belly laughed for the first time in ages. Bradley covered his mouth and cackled. It was so unusual to see his face so bright and so much different than the solemn kid he found in the room in D.C.

"You mean your adopted dad, don't you?" Owen said. They both laughed out loud again. The waitress shook her head and walked away.

Chapter Sixteen

Robert Swag walked into Henry's bar in Jersey City, a wide Bandaid barely covered the split on his forehead, and a black half-moon circle beneath his right eye. The bartender was leaning forward with both hands flat on the bar. "Nice knowin' ya, Bobby," he chuckled. "What do ya mean by that, Henry?" Swag said gruffly. Henry nodded towards the dark corner in the back of the bar. Carlos Triano was sitting stiffly upright staring at Swag. "Oh, shit," Swag said softly as he took a step in Triano's direction.

The trip from the bar to Triano seemed like forever, but not long enough to suit Swag. He bit his lip and tried to come up with a good line, but his nerves kept him from thinking about anything acceptable.

"What's up, boss?" he asked meekly.

"Sit down, Bobby."

"About that thing, boss…"

"Shut up and listen, Bobby." Triano snapped. Swag stopped in an instant and waited.

"The other families are laughing at us, Bobby. You capped a guy who owed us ninety thousand dollars and what did you get out of it? A worthless piece of paper. When somebody gets capped like that the cops come sniffin' around and no tellin' what they dig up. It's a concern for the whole organization. You say them other papers them guys have are worth millions, but we don't know if they're worth nothin' at all. And besides that, you didn't even get the other pages."

"Boss…"

"Shut up, Bobby. Don't talk!"

"Do you know who Ricky Costa is? He's Tony Costello's nephew. He's Tony's sister's kid. What the fuck! He's got a broken arm and a busted eyebrow. What am I gonna tell Tony? Do I say, Tony, John Wilkes Booth had a missin' diary and the top muscle in my organization can't get it from a couple-a amateur stooges?"

"What do ya want me to do, boss?" Swag said quietly.

"I want you to find them motherfuckers and cap both of' em!"

"You sayin' to kill 'em?"

"I'm saying kill both of 'em, Bobby. Both 'em"

Swag left Henry's without another word. He needed to find out if Owen and Bradley were still in town. By now they would have learned they were dealing with heavy hitters and moved to a safer location. He needed to round up a crew, but he was old school and didn't use cell phones or e-mail. The Feds monitored that shit all the time and there wasn't a pay phone anywhere. Back in the old days he would have rung up a pay phone in one of the bars in Newark, and would have something put together in fifteen minutes. Now the only safe thing to do was to make personal contact.

Owen and Bradley were back on the road. They were south of Chattanooga, Tennessee, still in the mountains in Georgia. After thinking about their situation for several hours, Owen's mind dodging through time, navigating his past memories, and wondering about his future, he decided to head south. He had a friend, Pete Findley, a guy he served with in Afghanistan who lived in Bon Secour, Alabama, a small town among a cluster of small towns on the Gulf Coast. They had stayed in touch while Owen was in Leesville, and he was a man who could be counted on. When Owen suggested heading to the Gulf coast, Bradley's answer was, "Okay."

Owen drove all night. He was exhausted but getting a hotel room wasn't an option. He had saved a considerable amount of money because he and Bradley had been living like hermits. Sending money to Susan to support the girls was more important than sleeping in a comfortable bed for one night. Bradley was satisfied napping in the passenger seat. That carefree feeling Owen experienced while living in D.C. was still lingering in the back of his mind. He didn't really believe the mob was after him, instead he thought he and Bradley were victims of mistaken identity. It would be easy enough to get labeled for something you didn't do when you were living in one room with another guy where there were probably past occupants who were involved in illegal activity. After thinking it over the original tension he experienced had lessoned considerably. He would be cautious, but he wasn't going to let it dominate his life.

Leaving D.C. was more like, well, *there's nothing left to lose.*

In reality, that wasn't the case. Robert Swag was going to locate Owen and Bradley and kill them. His problem was that they were going to be hard to find. He didn't like using modern technology, but he contacted Vinney to search Owen Black on the internet. Vinney found that Owen was a decorated war hero, and that his hometown was Leesville, Kentucky. Owen had been receiving paychecks from Wilson Construction Company, a Leesville based construction company. Owen's wife was still living there, teaching at a local elementary school.

Swag put together a three-man team; four counting himself. The main reason was the number was right to fit into the Cadillac comfortably.

Swag's intention was to find Susan Black and get Owen's location from her. He would torture her if it was necessary, but if he could find another way he would. Swag was a veteran in savagery; it didn't bother him to exact pain on others, but involving additional people meant leaving a wider trail. He never took public transportation or used a credit card. He always drove the Cadillac and carried a boatload of cash. It was over eight hundred miles from Jersey City to Leesville, he would have to fill the car at least twice, but he didn't intend to make food stops. He stocked the Caddy with four buckets of Kentucky Fried Chicken, six liters of Mountain Dew, and 2 gallons of water. The guys laughed about eating Kentucky Fried Chicken on their way to Kentucky. Swag laughed too.

Robert Swag was never credited with being the brightest man in the dumb row, but he was careful, and he was the most ruthless individual who ever drove down the pike. Swag had put so many people into their graves that he'd lost track of them all. So far he had avoided being convicted of anything more serious than extortion and racketeering. He always stayed true to the organization, keeping his mouth shut and he had taken the fall when they put the squeeze on him. Because of that he was one of the most valued mobsters on the east coast. Yet, in spite of that, there was a problem looming. Arthur Sweeney was an intolerable human being, a loser, and a man without a backbone, but he was brilliant. Sweeney would lay some real problems at Swag's feet even from the grave.

Swag and his men left chicken bones all along the highway from New Jersey to Kentucky, but they made it with only two stops for fuel. They never used the rest area restrooms, but instead ventured into the woods past the dog walks for relief. Swag theorized there were security cameras in the main lobbies of every rest area in America, and he wasn't wrong.

Susan Black's home was easy to find in Leesville. She was still working when they got there and her doors were unlocked like most people in town. Swag and his three companions simply walked in and started searching everything. They found an overnight package from Owen from D.C. with a cashier's check for two thousand dollars, and a note telling her that he was heading south to hook up with Pete. Several unopened letters were in a dresser drawer labeled Pete Findley. Swag opened them all and read them.

Pete described where he was working and made several invitations for Owen to come down so they could "get on a terror," but the letters never specified his location. Obviously, he had disclosed that to Owen in previous communications.

Swag broke two of his own rules when he purchased a throw-away phone at Walmart and called Vinney to search for Pete Findley. Walmart has security cameras, and even though Vinney also used throw away phones, Swag suspected the Feds knew the pings from Sorrento's restaurant like the backs of their hands. The good news was that Vinney had an address for Pete Findley in Bon Secour, Alabama.

Owen and Bradley left Interstate 10 at the Bay Minette exit east of Mobile, Alabama and headed south through Daphne and Fairhope, staying on the scenic route along the bay to Bon Secour. Bradley was fascinated by the Spanish moss hanging in the live oaks, the palm trees strewn among the heavy underbrush, and the jungle-like plant life on both sides of the two-lane highway. He had been to Virginia Beach a few times before his mother died, but he had never seen anything like the gold coast of Alabama. Although his mother could have afforded extensive travel, or anything else she wanted, she was a very private person and chose to stay in Charlottesville exclusively, and as result Bradley had never seen most of the country. Now as a twenty-two year-old he was left with a flutter in his stomach as they ventured down the secluded highway into the unknown.

Pete Findley was working for Shelly's Seafood Supply Company located on Oster Bay on a dead-end gravel road.

At night the lights from Mobile outlined the city's skyline in the distance, with the black shadows of trees and brush against the pothole laden parking lot behind it. Shelly's could not have been more rustic looking even by design. The faded green metal exterior was dotted with blotches of rust, reams of fishnet, broken oars and a nautical wheel. A short pier and a boat slip extended into the bay where several dilapidated shrimp and fishing boats had found their final resting place.

It was evening when Owen and Bradley arrived. Pete was just getting off work and he didn't know Owen was coming. He walked towards them, the evening sun in his eyes and a long shadow was cast across the parking lot. Two other men who were with him split for their cars, but Pete walked straight ahead. The tall thin frame, the black graying hair, and an air of confidence in his gate was reminiscent of a "Marlboro Man" commercial from the seventies. Pete looked a lot like Sam Elliott when Sam was in his late thirties. He squinted, eyeballing Owen as he stepped out of the truck with the sunshine beaming over his shoulder. Owen's face was still obscured by the sunlight but when he took a few forward steps, Pete recognized his stride. A broad smile stretched across his face. He said, "Well, you old warrior! It's about time!" He threw his arms around Owen and pounded his back.

"Pete, it's been too long," Owen said.

"You got that right, brother," Pete said.

Several minutes were consumed comparing their present appearance to what they looked like a few years back. Both insisting that the other had not changed much with age. Owen introduced Bradley, and the trip from D.C. was discussed. Pete was surprised. He had no idea Owen had left Leesville.

Pete's home was a rusty twenty-five feet trailer house hidden in the weeds and brush across the parking lot from Shelly's. It was attached to a small pavilion with a picnic table, a small refrigerator and a hammock. Pete had hung lights and installed a shower and a free-standing sink in the pavilion. He slept outside in the hammock more than in his bed.

Owen wasn't shocked at all about Pete's living conditions, but he was curious. Pete graduated in the top ten percent of his class from LSU with a Bachelor of Science degree before joining the military. He could do many things with his hands and his mind and although this suited his personality, Owen thought he might have wanted more.

After several Land Shark beers Owen gave up the details of his pending divorce, his failed attempt to reinstate in the military, and finally the facts about being attacked in their apartment in D.C. Pete listened with a placid expression, but after hearing the details of the attack he said, "I'll bet they got their asses handed to them," and then he laughed loudly. Bradley shook his head in agreement.

"We don't know who they were or what they have against us, but when somebody comes calling with a double-barreled shotgun you have to get a little serious," Owen said.

"You got that right, brother," Pete said.

"Sean, our bartender, thinks they were with the mob," Bradley said.

"Why?"

"My dad owed them some money. I think they killed him, and maybe they were after me too,"

"That's crazy. Have they asked you for money?"

"No."

"That's probably not it then. If they wanted money, they wouldn't be trying to kill you, would they?" Pete said.

Bradley smiled slightly. Probably not, but what do they want?"

"They must have mistaken us for someone else," Owen said.

They all sat silently for a long time, each within their own thoughts. Finally, Pete said, "Okay, what now. Where do we go from here.?

I need to work," Owen said. "My girls are in a private school, and Susan doesn't make enough money to keep things together without a steady income from me."

"These aren't the best of times, but there's plenty of work around here. Construction companies need employees building boat slips, decks and stuff like that," Pete said.

"I don't know how to build anything," Owen said. Bradley hesitated for a moment and then said," I know how to build things."

"You know how to build things?" Owen asked with raised eyebrows.

"Yes, I know how to build things."

Owen smiled. Bradley never ceased to amaze him. "How?" He asked.

"My trigonometry professor in boarding school wanted us to be able to apply what we learned in school to real life. He made us build things. We made models of homes, bridges and even skyscrapers. Building big things is the same as building small things mathematically."

Owen left the picnic table and dropped into the hammock. He had been awake for more than twenty-four hours. He was exhausted. The last words he uttered before he slipped into sleep were, "Okay, then. Tomorrow we look for work building things."

Pete finished his beer, went inside the trailer and returned with a roll of blankets. Daytime temperatures in December on the Gulf were in the mid-sixties but at night it dropped down into the forties. Bradley approached Owen, glanced meekly at Pete and then carefully removed Owen's shoes. Pete smiled. "Don't be embarrassed about taking care of your friend. He'd do the same for you," he said.

As he headed off to bed he added, "You get the couch."

Chapter Seventeen

Robert Swag grunted as he pushed himself from the Caddy out into the bright morning sunlight. He had stopped behind an abandoned Sinclair gas station where he slept for two hours. His three companions were each slumped against a car door with the windows down snorting and snoring in their sleep. Swag waded into the weeds and relieved himself. He walked back to the car and opened his Atlas onto the car hood. With a yellow marker he lined out a route to Orange Beach, Alabama. Mario, one of his tree companions got out of the car and joined him. "Bobby, you need a GPS," he said.

"We don't need no GPS. If you've been using one of them things and the Feds get ahold of it, they can tell every place you been. Did ya know that, Mario?"

"No, I didn't. I didn't know that, Bobby."

"Well you need to know things," Swag said as he folded up the Atlas. "Get them guys up and take a piss, cause I ain't stopping until we get to Mobile. Mario was quick to do as he was told and in minutes they were on the road again. They had driven through the night from Leesville to Nashville, and then south on I-59 to Birmingham before Swag got off onto a country road for a pit stop and those few hours of rest. The plan was to get to Orange Beach where Vinney had arranged to have them put up in a home owned by one of

Carlos Triano's mobster buddies. From there they would locate Owen and Bradley, construct a plan, and an escape route. Swag would kill them both because that was what he was ordered to do, but he wanted to get John Wilkes Booth's diary too. He wanted to redeem himself in the eyes of the boss.

When they arrived in Gulf Shores, Alabama, it was mid-afternoon. The traffic on Beach Road was light as Swag headed east. The City of Orange Beach connected with Gulf Shores and only the locals knew when you were in one or the other. The sky was clear, the waves marching onto the beach were carrying a white foam on the sway as sunlight glistened through the emerald green water.

"Let's stop and look at the beach, Bobby," Mario said.

"I wanna get to that house and crack open a bottle a wine, and maybe have some pasta and meatballs delivered. Besides that, you've seen plenty of the ocean in Jersey," Swag said.

"There ain't no women in swimming suits in Jersey, Bobby."

Swag thought for a long moment before he started speaking. "Did I ever tell any of you about the first time I seen the ocean?" Swag asked. Nobody answered.

"When I was a kid, livin' down in Hells Kitchen, my old man came home after he'd been out all night with his friends. My ma was hanging clothes out on the line in the back yard. Ma asked him where he'd been and he slapped her so hard that he bloodied her nose and blacked both her eyes. The next morning early, my grandfather, Papa Mike Corgliano come over with two of his guys. He put my dad in the car and he let me go along with him. They drove over to New York Harbor and took my dad out in a little boat. Papa Mike left me on the dock and told me not to go anywhere. When he come back my dad wasn't with them. I asked, where is my dad. Papa Mike said, he's sleepin' with the fishees. That was the first time I ever heard that said, and it was the first time I ever seen the ocean."

It was quiet. It was as though Swag's three companions were afraid to draw a breath but then Swag laughed. "He was sleepin' with the fishees!" The car erupted with laughter. When Mario caught his breath he said, "Bobby, that wasn't the ocean, that was the harbor." It was quiet again.

While Swag was reminiscing about his father's demise, he cruised through a set of amber flashing lights. A man caught in the crosswalk shouted angrily. Swag shouted back, "I'm drivin' here!" He didn't realize he was required to yield to pedestrians. As a result, in just a few moments red and blue flashing lights were closing in on him. The police officer schooled Swag regarding amber flashing lights in a crosswalk, and then issued a traffic citation. As soon as the squad car drove away Swag pitched the ticket out the window.

At 5:00 a.m., that same day, back in the weeds in the pavilion, bacon was cooking, the aroma mingling with the smell of the sea air; Pete was stirring up breakfast for his guest. Owen opened his eyes, rubbed his face and started looking around. Pete was standing over the flat iron gas grill with a spatula in his hand. "Food is always better when its cooked outside," he said.

"Smells good," Owen said, stretching and yawning, and finally maneuvering out of the hammock. It was still dark and stars were visible in the sky.

"Got you a job," Pete said nonchalantly.

"No way."

"Yep, Shelly needs repairs on the dock. Is tomorrow morning too soon?"

"No! Today's not too soon, but how did you do that?

"Shelly gets to the office at about 3:00 a.m. I just walked over there and asked," Pete said, turning an egg over on the grill.

"Tell her we're ready anytime. Right now if she needs us, Owen said.

"Tomorrow will be fine, Owen, but Shelly is a dude. He's a Viet Nam vet. When I told him you were a Navy Seal he couldn't wait to say yes. How about Bradley?" Pete asked.

"Pete, I never knew a more congenial guy. I think he'll be grateful."

Bradley made his entrance as Pete was dishing out the grub. He walked over to the grill and asked if he could help. Pete said, "I got it, kid, have a seat."

"We're going to work for Shelly, Owen said.

"Okay. Are we gonna peel shrimp?" Bradley asked, not taking even a moment to consider the offer.

"No, we're going to fix the dock."

"Okay."

With that said, breakfast was consumed. Owen thanked Pete for opening his trailer and pavilion to them and his hospitality. Pete laughed stating that it wasn't exactly the Hilton suites, but it was home. Owen wasn't judgmental about how Pete was living, but he was curious. How could he be critical of Pete when he was only a few paychecks away from being homeless himself.

As Pete cleaned the picnic table he seemed somewhere far away. Finally, he said "Sam killed himself up in St. Louis, Owen."

"I heard that, Pete. Shipley too, out in Arizona," Owen said, quietly.

"I took Shelly up to Birmingham about a month ago to the Veteran's hospital and I saw Carl Slingerland on a corner with a cardboard box on his chest. WILL WORK FOR FOOD. He had a beard and his hair was long and tangled; his face dirty. I didn't recognize him until we made eye contact. He recognized me too, but he turned away. I haven't been able to stop thinking about him," Pete said.

"What about you, Pete?" Owen asked.

"I'm good, Owen. I like working here. I Like Shelly. I've got a girl half my age too, but I know that's going nowhere;

she's pretty, and smart – too smart to stick around with an old dude like me, so I'm keeping it cool. We go out a few times a month and she stays overnight sometimes. Yea, I'm okay. This is what I want. I'm happy."

Pete didn't ask Owen. It was obvious things had gone seriously downhill for him, but Pete wasn't worried about Owen. He had always been stable and sane. Owen didn't have a serious explanation for where he was going or how he would get over the slump he was in, but in an effort to get past talking about the sad demise of former colleagues he said, "Pete, If I ever win the lotto, I'm going to Alaska. I'll build a lodge, get a couple of fishing boats, and be a tour guide. I'll use the skills I learned in the Seals to run a search and rescue operation on the side."

"What do you know about Alaska?"

"Nothing, but I can learn.

A mixture of rain and snow was falling on Washington, D.C., as dusk descended on the city. It was six thirty, the lights were still shining on the third floor of the FBI field office. Lee Ford and Tyrese Jefferson were in Lee's office. Tyrese was slouching in a chair, his coat unbuttoned, his tie hung loosely around his neck, and a coffee mug in his hand. Lee was upright behind his desk, his brow furrowed, a frown across his face.

"Margaret is still working downstairs. She just sent this e-mail. Guess who's on the internet again, looking for Owen Black?"

"Uh, the mob?"

"Right on, buddy. There was a ping out of Leesville, Kentucky, to Sorrento's from a throw-away, and then immediately after that activity started on the web. They're looking at a guy by the name of Pete Findley in Bon Secour, Alabama. He's an old war buddy of Black's."

Just then Tyrese got a ping. A text message from the communications sergeant in the district notifying him that Robert Swag was ticketed for blowing a crosswalk in Gulf Shores, Alabama.

"Wow, that's magic," Tyrese said, handing the phone to Lee.

"Lee looked at it. "Go home, get some rest. I have a feeling we're taking a little trip in the morning."

Tyrese smiled. "We might just have a real case here, Lee, even if you did lose Edward Snowden."

"Not funny." Lee said.

Robert Swag was rich by any standard, all by ill-gotten gains, but he lived a very modest existence. He had a three-room apartment in Newark, decorated nineteen seventies style, and stocked with the original furniture he purchased when he moved in during the early eighties. Any reasonable accommodations were sufficient for him, so when he pulled into the driveway at 2723 Marina Road, in Orange Beach to see a small brick ranch style home shaded by a stand of live oak trees, flush with Spanish moss, brush and wild grass abundant enough to conceal a colony of rabbits, he wasn't disappointed. His three associates weren't as easily satisfied.

"This is it? Are you kidding me!" Mario spouted, leaving no doubt in his tone that he wasn't pleased. Sal Lomilino, a lower level hood who was working his way up the ladder was next to express his disappointment. "You'd think a wise guy from Manhattan could do a little better than this," he said. The third guy, Frank Fortillo, was silent.

Swag popped open the Cadillac's trunk and retrieved his bag. He pitched the other bags onto the ground with a thud. "You guys need to shut your mouths. I know you from the neighborhood. I knew your parents. None of you ever lived in a place as good as this. I ain't even seen the inside of this but I know it's better than any a yous had. So shut your fuckin' lip!"

They continued into the house. Swag was on a terror as he approached the door. He flung the keys at Sal. "Open the fuckin' door!"

"Okay, Bobby, cool it, we're all good here."

"You guys need to listen and look at things. Ain't none a you looked at nothin' since we got here. You just want to see the beach. Did you see these people, they're all dressed in them bright shirts with parrots and birds a-paradise and things like that, and they wear big baggy shorts with more pockets than a pool-table. The old guys wear big white shoes and white socks and their fat wives got on them shiny tight silky knee pants that shows every roll and wrinkle they got. We need to fit in!"

When they got inside Swag marched through the house examining everything. "There's three ways out of here, the kitchen, the front door and that sliding door off the main bedroom, if you don't count the windows. This road we're on is Marina Drive. It's named right but it's a stupid place to have a house in our business. We're on a dead-end road, and we're surrounded by water, but yous didn't notice that. All you seen was that it wasn't beautiful!"

"Bobby, it's alright!" Sal said.

"No, it ain't alright. You three all got cell phones. I told you before we started that we ain't talking on no cell phone. I seen Mario in the back seat fiddling with that damn thing!"

"I was playing a game, Bobby. I wasn't talking on it."

"It don't matter. The Feds know where cells phones are and who's got 'em. It's just lucky that Mario ain't important enough for them to key in on him." Swag stopped for a moment and glared at all three. "I want them Goddamn cells phones put up in that drawer until we leave here." He pointed to a dresser in the hallway to the bathroom.

"Okay, Bobby. You're the boss," Sal said turning his hands out.

Mario plucked his cell phone from his pocket, walked down the hallway and pitched it into the drawer. The other two followed suite.

Chapter Eighteen

In less than two days Shelly's dock and pier had a new look. In those places where the old boards were replaced with new gave the pier an appearance of a huge piano keyboard. Shelly asked Bradley to install built-in benches, one facing east and the other to the west. As the sun was dipping below the tree line Bradley was putting on the finishing touches. Owen had put the tools away, and now sat dangling his legs off the dock, watching Bradley skillfully cutting out cup holders in the armrests.

"I sent Wilson a note before we left D.C. last week explaining our sudden departure. I asked them to send our paychecks to Susan in Leesville. Is that okay with you?"

Bradley finished the cupholder with sandpaper and then blew off the dust. "Okay," he said.

Shelly sauntered up the pier with his hands in his pockets. Shelly was a businessman, but he looked more like he might have ventured out of a mountain cave. His long gray hair covered his ears, wild bushy eyebrows were like two brushes fixed above his eyes. He wore bib overalls, scuffed brogan shoes and a faded Harley Davidson t-shirt.

"The benches are beautiful. Now I can watch the sun set and rise over creation while I sit here in my little part of the world, he said. His voice was coarse, his speech low and calming. "You boys do good work, but I don't have any more carpenter work, but if you like peeling shrimp and cleaning up fish guts you can stick around for a while."

"Do you really need us?" Owen asked.

"Right now I've got seven guys. I get by with that, but most don't last long. It won't hurt to have a man or two in reserve."

"We'll work for minimum wage," Owen said. Bradley was shaking his head in agreement.

"Hell no!" Shelly said. "You're worth more than that. I pay seventeen bucks an hour and that's really not enough."

Owen smiled. Shelly really was a magnificent soul.

They had been staying with Pete, and when they suggested they were looking for cheap lodging Pete couldn't hide his disappointment. "This place is a dump, but it's free," he would say. The truth was that Owen loved it there. Sleeping in the hammock with the smell of the sea air, hanging out under the moonlight and a star-studded sky was as close to heaven as you could get. It was like living in a parallel reality.

To celebrate their semi-permanent employment, Pete offered to spring for a few beers. They drove to Orange Beach to The FloraBama Lounge, found it too crowded, so they continued on to a more secluded local watering hole, Pleasure Island Tiki Bar. It was a small place with a pier, boat slips, and a regular crowd. When they entered the bartender acknowledged Pete with a wave and broad smile. They found a table on the deck where they could watch the boat traffic on the bay. Owen thought it wasn't much different than Pete's place, minus the weeds and brush and his rusty old trailer. Of course, Pete's pavilion was flush with fishing poles, nets, oars, and Shelly's Seafood Company was hulking over the parking lot.

As they settled in, a couple who looked totally out of place sauntered through the bar and then took the steps downstairs to the bags game court. Most people in the south call the game "cornhole." Small bags are filled with beans or corn kernels to be tossed at a board with a hole in it. Points are scored when an individual on one end of the court pitches the bag through the hole. It alternates between the players on each end until a certain amount of points is scored. The game leaves little to fight about. The bag either goes through the hole or it doesn't.

The man was about thirty, slightly overweight, long brown greasy hair and wearing ill-fitting jeans and a Harley Davidson t-shirt. His companion was about the same age. She was thin, bleached blond hair with roots showing, a round stomach not proportionate to the rest of her body. She was wearing a bright yellow blouse and knee length leggings. Although it was mid-December the temperature was in the mid-sixties. The crowd on the deck was dressed in shorts and t-shirts or light sweaters. They were locals who were retired, vacationers, or people like Pete who were employed along the coast.

It was easy to see that the pair didn't fit in. The man's name was Charley and the woman, Tammy. They didn't immediately begin playing cornhole but they were definitely interested. It was as though they didn't know what it was. Tammy took off her shoes and kicked sand around but finally picked up one of the bags, eyeballed the hole in the board and pitched it, missing by several feet. Charley laughed.

They put their heads together analyzing the situation until they came up with a concept. They each took an end, each pitching the bags in an attempt to hit the hole. Tammy scored first, and then again. Charley decided the game wasn't worth playing so he pretended a jump shot. He did that several times before Tammy had had enough. She picked up a bag and fired it at Charley overhand. Charley ducked as the bag whizzed past his ear.

One of the older women on the deck said, "Look at that, they're fighting." Several other people peeked over the railing to take a look. Tammy walked to Charley's end of the court and pushed him. Charley laughed. Tammy giggled, and pushed him again. Charley grasped Tammy's hands, holding them down as she giggled and squirmed to get free. Charley let go and tried to hug her. Tammy relented her pushing and hugged him back. An older guy on the deck said, "Yep, they're fighting alright."

Tammy went back to her end and picked up her bags. Charley tossed a bag with just enough zip on it to scare her, barely missing her leg. Tammy ran at Charley, still giggling, but swinging with a little more gusto. Charley held her arms again until she stopped struggling. This time Charley wasn't smiling.

Someone on the deck said, "That's ridiculous." The rest of the crowd had stopped eating and watched, amused by the development. Charley left the court, heading towards the pier. Tammy stamped her foot, but after a few seconds she followed him. A meticulously dressed little woman in her seventies said, "Look, he's taking one of the bags." The rest of the crowd hummed with disgust.

Tammy caught up with Charley, put her arm around his waist as they sauntered down the pier. There was a boat docked with a man on the third deck apparently gathering his gear to put the boat away for the day. Charley stopped and looked up at him. Whatever went through Charley's mind is unknown, but after some consideration he hurled the bag at the man with everything he had in him. The guy ducked, took a moment to analyze what had happened, and then threw the bag back at Charley. Both men stared at the other with contempt. The gathering on the deck oohed and awed in amazement.

Charley picked up the bag; he and Tammy walked to the end of the pier arm in arm. It was dusk, the sky was clear above but clouds in the distance were illuminated periodically by lightning. Boats with tourist were entering the bay at the end of the pier. In his final act of brilliance Charley tried to hit a duck boat full of people with the cornhole bag as it motored past the pier. He missed by several feet and the bag plunged into the water. Everybody on the dock was watching.

Owen, Pete, and Bradley were as enthralled as the others. "It takes all kinds of people to make a world," Pete said. Bradley smiled. Owen chuckled softly.

When Charley and Tammy came past the dock headed to the parking lot, they were holding hands. An older man stood up declaring loudly, "We could play cornhole but somebody threw the damn bag into the ocean!"

There were four men leaning over the rail watching Charley and Tammy disappearing into the shadows of the parking lot. All four were wearing new colorful shirts, and baggy cargo shorts. A heavy- set man in the middle was wearing a bright yellow Hawaiian shirt with palm trees prominently across his chest. His socks were knee length, and his shoes were as white as new-fallen snow. It was Robert Swag.

Owen was still smiling when he looked up to see Swag. A cold chill ran through him as Swag continued to watch Charley and Tammy. He was laughing just as Owen had laughed. Was it possible this was the same shotgun-toting criminal who had tried to kill him in Washington, D.C.? There are only so many faces in the world to go around, and it was possible this guy was just an innocent tourist watching a man make a fool of himself. His face was so similar that it was unnerving.

Owen nudged Bradley. "Does that guy look familiar to you?"

Bradley studied Swag for a moment. "No."

"He looks a lot like the guy who tried to kill us," Owen said.

"I only saw the back of his head when I hit him with the computer."

Pete listened, observing the conversation and watching Swag. "Do we confront him or call the cops?

Owen thought about it for a long moment. "I don't know, Pete. He looks something like the guy, but I'm not sure."

Swag and his companions were stone-cold killers, but if Owen and Pete confronted them and found resistance there was only one way it would turn out. Four wise guys from Jersey would be getting patched up at the local hospital. Neither Pete nor Owen talked about what they had been through in Afghanistan but there was nothing in civilian life that could compare with it. Taking on four men at a beachside restaurant would be nothing more than child's play.

"With no more evidence than we have, going to the police won't work," Pete said.

"Let's get out of here. We'll keep an eye on them. If they follow us, we'll know," Owen said.

Bradley's brow furrowed, and his lips tightened. "What do they want? Do they want money? Does Arthur – my dad owe them money? If that's what they want, I'll give them money," he said.

"Bradley, if that's what they want they wouldn't be trying to kill you. You can't get money from a dead man. It has to be something else," Pete said. It was the same thing he had said before, and it made sense. The reality was that Swag had embarrassed his boss with the nonsense regarding John Wilkes Booth's diary, and now Owen and Bradley were slated to pay for it. Pete, too, if he got in the way. The irony was that Swag still wanted those seventeen pages of paper and all he had to do to get it was to find Owen's truck, open the door and take it from behind the seat. He would also be reunited with his last murder victim who was still taking up space in an urn sitting on top of those seventeen pages.

After a short discussion Owen decided he would walk right past Swag to gauge his reaction. Pete and Bradley would follow him. If they didn't see anything unusual – no prolonged looks, or suspicious quiet conversations between the four men, they would reassess the situation. If they were followed they would deal with them in an appropriate manner.

As Owen walked by Swag, he leaned in and bumped him slightly. "Oh, I'm sorry," he said. Swag said, "No problem." Owen smiled as he examined Swag's features. Swag smiled making it more difficult to make the assessment. When he last saw Swag, his face was gnarled in hatred and strained in preparation for getting his head split open. He looked different. So much so that Owen didn't think Swag was the guy.

Owen, Bradley and Pete proceeded to the truck and drove away. The lane to Pleasure Island Tiki Bar was dark and there were no car lights following them. Owen was open to the thought that he was just imagining things.

Swag and his entourage got up to leave the bar, each carrying a plastic cup containing beer. As they headed down the ramp the bartender said, "Hey, guys, you can't leave the bar carrying open alcohol."

Swag said, "Go fuck yourself!"

Sal turned up his cup, guzzled his beer, and then pitched the cup onto the floor. "There you go, I'm all legal now."

As they walked through the parking lot Swag said, "I been thinkin'. That guy that bumped me. He resembled that Owen Black."

"You mean the Owen Black we're supposed to off?" Mario asked.

"Yea, that guy."

"What are the odds, Bobby. We go out for a drink to get outta that house for few hours and we bump into the guy we're supposed to kill? That ain't possible." Sal said.

"You're probably right, Sal," Swag said, turning up his cup to finish his beer.

Chapter Nineteen

Owen, Bradley and Pete were quiet on the ride home. They were considering the situation from their own individual point of view. Bradley was still trying to find a way to blame himself for everything, although at that point nothing had actually happened. Pete was protective, already thinking in that engrained military modality – gain a superior vantage point in order to attack or dig in to defend a position. Owen was least concerned. There wasn't anything between heaven and earth that he had done to have the mob stalking him for a kill. But still, ten years in country had implanted a deep-rooted respect for caution.

It was nine p.m.. A slight breeze was blowing in across the bay; lightning in the clouds out in the ocean glowing red and white, billowing skyward into the night. Shelly was sitting on one of his new benches with his arms crossed looking out at sea. Owen parked the truck and all three men walked out onto the pier to join him.

"Are you sleeping here tonight?" Pete asked.

"Naw, just watching Mother Nature putting on a show," he said.

"You might as well stay, you'll be back before three." Pete said

"I would if I thought that storm out there was coming in. I love the sound of rain on that tin roof, but it's going east. I'll watch it for a while anyway."

Shelly had a fold out bed in the office. It wasn't unusual for him to sleep over several nights in a row. Owen wanted Shelly to know about their possible mob sighting. If there really was trouble ahead he didn't want Shelly blindsided. He suggested that maybe he and Bradley should find another place to stay. Shelly crossed his arms and leaned back to look again at the lightning on the horizon. His voice soft and low, he said, "Owen, that would hurt me if you did that."

That was the end of the conversation.

On the fourth floor of the FBI Washington D.C. field office, Lee Ford and Tyrese Jefferson were going over the information they had on Owen and Bradley. As things were coming together, the farce they were assigned to investigate was actually developing into something interesting. Everything they had was circumstantial, but solid. Lee was beginning to believe the joke was on the Bureau. The Art Crime Division usually handled illegal possession of cultural artifacts, but they probably passed on this case believing it was equivalent to chasing down a UFO siting. That being the situation, it was easy to punish Lee with it. Now that the case had legs, Lee was analyzing the evidence with a different slant.

"I wish we had the evidence the police collected at the Arthur Sweeney crime scene," Lee said, as he scanned through the reports the D.C Police had provided.

"They gave us everything they had, didn't they?" Tyrese said.

"Yes, but murder isn't a federal crime. They get to process everything at the D.C. crime lab. I wish we had all that stuff down at Quantico. I'd like to see every file in that computer back-doored by somebody who knows what they're doing."

"A federal judge could order them to give it to us," Tyrese said.

"True enough, we've got probable cause to think a federal gambling violation has been committed, but I really don't want to piss the guys off in the district. I know this case is starting to get momentum, but as far as they're concerned, they have a murder investigation, and we have a cultural artifact case."

"Maybe we could just ask them politely," Tyrese said.

Lee rubbed his chin. "Maybe we could."

With that said, they moved on to another subject; Going to Gulf Shores, Alabama to follow up on Robert Swag's presence there. Lee had updated John Wodetski on how the John Wilkes Booth diary farce had manifested into so much more. Murder wasn't a federal crime, but murder by someone involved in syndicated gambling in order to collect a debt was a violation of the federal RECO Act. Wodetski was skeptical, but agreed to give Lee latitude to follow up on it. However, when he asked for the use of the FBI Lear Jet, Wodetski laughed in his face. Therefore, he and Tyrese would be driving to Gulf Shores.

In the interim Lee sent a text message to D.C. police asking them politely if the FBI could take Sweeney's computer to the federal crime lab at Quantico. He knew he wouldn't get an immediate response, but he had set things in motion.

Robert Swag was nervous about searching for info on a computer but continued to stay in contact with Vinney back at Sorrento's in Manhattan against his better judgement. Vinney provided an address for Pete Findley, and pictures of Shelly's Seafood Company, along with Pete's house trailer, the pavilion, and maps of the gulf coast - all from Google Earth. Swag had the information faxed to a Fed Ex store in Fulton.

It was impossible to rent a boat anywhere along the coast without providing personal information and a credit card, so Swag bought a small motorized catamaran from a junk boat dealer with cash after being assured it was seaworthy. It wasn't anything to look at, and four passengers would be a little snug on board that little boat, but Swag wasn't interested in sailing the seven seas. He just wanted something capable of negotiating the coast well enough to get from Stanley's Marina at Swift's Landing in Oyster Bay to Shelly's Seafood Company.

The road to Shelly's was a dead end with heavy brush and trees on one side and the bay on the other. The fact that there was only one way out worried Swag. An escape by boat was the only sensible resolution. Sal had a boat of his own back in Jersey so he was designated operator. Still Swag's philosophy was never "depend on anyone – never trust anyone." In that vein he tried several dry runs from Oyster Bay to Shelly's. He took control of the helm on two occasions himself. Sal convinced Swag to purchase a GPS capable of navigating on water with assurance that he would deposit it in the sea when they were clear.

When they returned to the house after everything was set, Swag continually lectured the others on the art of assassination. "Taking somebody out in Alabama ain't the same as taking them out in Jersey. We've got protection in Jersey. We ain't got even one dirty cop in Alabama, and we ain't got a single politician in our pocket," he said, popping the cork on a bottle of Antinori Antinanello. He sipped a small portion and then poured a glass for each of the others.

"When you're taking somebody out you got to have the right tools. You see them blacks down in the slums shooting all over the place with them AR-15's and them short little automatics. They kill more people that don't have nothin' to do with business than them that do." He walked over to the dresser where he had placed his Winchester sawed-off shotgun. He snapped it open showing the buckshot in the chamber. This right here will do some real damage, and it don't spit out any empty cartridges like them pump shotguns. Now sometimes when you got more targets in a room and there's only you, you have to use a pump, but it's better if you can just take this double barrel sawed-off Winchester in to do the job. When you're done you don't hafta go around picking up shell casings."

"Bobby, do you ever use a handgun?" Sal asked.

"I have, but I use a .357 magnum, and I do that for the same reason. It don't spit out no shells. Sometimes when I got to get into a place where it's a little tight, I use a .38 snub-nose with hollow-points. When one of them babies goes in it don't come out."

"Why don't you just tape the handle with duct tape and wipe it down and leave it, Bobby?" Mario asked.

"'Cause you don't know if you're gonna get in a corner somewhere before you're clear and you gotta shoot your way out. You can't do that with just your pecker in your hand," he laughed. The others laughed too. "Guns ain't as easy to get these days. I like to keep my guns cause they're clean. If I leave 'em at a scene I gotta get new guns and I ain't so sure where they been and who's keeping an eye on 'em.

It was late, Swag turned his wine glass up and emptied it as he headed for his bedroom. "Get some sleep," he said.

The lights went out at Shelly's at 8:45 p.m.. Shelly walked out on his pier to sit on his newly constructed built-in bench. Pete, Owen, Bradley and the other employees were out at 6:30, but Shelly always hung around, often just sitting in his office, or standing on the pier looking out to sea. Now he had a place to sit and "watch the sun set on creation."

The wreckage parked alongside Shelly's pier was a product of the times. Fishermen who were operating on a shoestring budget often found their fishing boats and shrimp boats damaged beyond repair, and when you were busted sometimes you just had to cut your losses and head off into the sunset. Sometimes they put in at Shelly's never to return. It was expensive to get those old wrecks out of the water, so Shelly was left with the problem of getting rid of them.

Every boat docked at Shelly's pier had a "Free," sign hanging on it somewhere. Sometimes trawlers down on their luck looking for parts to make repairs on their own boats made their way to Shelly's. Boats with parts strewn about the deck were left for Shelly to handle, but he never complained. Some of those salty old guys were strapped for time to get back out to sea, and sometimes their boats were marooned offshore waiting for rescue. Those guys were prone to leave a mess when they were in a hurry to get back to work.

It wasn't unusual for people to sneak in during the night to steal parts from those old pieces of junk. All they had to do was to ask, but either they didn't realize Shelly would let them have anything they could extract, or they were just plain stupid. He had seen a small catamaran prowling around in the darkness for the last few days. He thought theft might be the motivation. As kind-hearted and generous as he was, Shelly hated people who would rather steal than ask for help. If that catamaran was cruising the bay with larceny as the intent, Shelly was ready to help them expand their minds.

Pete came out of the darkness, clumping across the boards slowly, his silhouette visible in the moonlight. Shelly didn't even look up. He knew Pete's walk from a mile away. "What's up, Pete?" He asked.

"We're having a couple of nightcaps in the pavilion, maybe you could join us."

"Sure thing, but I'll be a few minutes. I've seen a little catamaran prowling around here the last couple of nights. I thought I'd check it out."

Pete looked out across the bay. He was as calm as a Sunday afternoon in a small town, but he had been a soldier for a good part of his life, and it had taken its toll. He was never caught with his pants down. His thoughts immediately went straight to calculating the possibility that it might have been those four men on the deck at the tiki bar. Still, he didn't want to jump to conclusions.

Owen was sitting at the picnic table and Bradley had carried out a small white cooler full of Land Shark beer. Lightning out over the Gulf periodically illuminated the clouds on the horizon. That part of Alabama is subtropical where rain is a frequent part of life, and people who live there are used to it. Shelly loved rain and lighting with billowing clouds out over the ocean. It was even more interesting to watch. As he sauntered across the parking lot his head tilted towards the heavens watching light streaking across the sky, his beard, wiry hair, and slender frame silhouetting in the darkness resembled a scarecrow walking across the parking lot. After walking down the pathway in the weeds to the pavilion, Pete was waiting with a Land Shark in his hand. "Here you go, you old warrior."

"Thank you, kid."

Pete was thirty nine years old, but he was a kid to Shelly. Shelly was seventy-four, going on eighty. Both men had been through a lot in their lives as did Owen. Bradley had traveled his own rocky road but in a different way. They were human warehouses of information, but none of them talked much about it. Pete and Owen often reminisced about conditions in Afghanistan; the extreme weather in the desert, and the mountain ranges where it often didn't rain for three months and the cold winters with eternal winds blowing down the mountainside. It was all fodder for conversation, but they hardly ever talked about Al-Quaeda, or the war. Shelly spoke about the monsoons in Viet Nam, but he was the same about what he had done in that God forsaken war. But still there were times when the subject ran a little deeper.

After several beers, Owen was a little chatty, deciding to reveal a memory he and Pete shared back in the day. He started with a chuckle, "Pete, do you remember when we were on patrol, clearing that little village east of Kabul?"

"Which one?" Pete asked, a puzzled expression on his face. Owen pretended to pull the trigger of a pistol rapidly. "Squirt, squirt," he said. Pete smiled," Yeah, I remember."

"We were checking out this house looking for Taliban. We really didn't think there was anything to the reports about suspicious activity because it was peaceful, and the people were so friendly. When Taliban's around you can't get a smile out of the villagers."

Shelly had his elbows on the table, a Landshark resting in his hand, smiling slightly. He knew Pete well enough to know there wouldn't be any blood and guts involved so he was relaxed.

"We were clearing this little house - we knocked on the door like we often did when we were just going through the motions. We yelled, we're coming in. This voice says, *Bia too,* in Dari, which means, come in. We were cautious but we really didn't expect anything, so I go inside and Pete follows me. This little old man was sitting on the floor on a

Persian rug with a little pink water gun in his hand. He's giggling like crazy as he's squirting us with a stream of water. At first we thought it might be a distraction, so we got serious in a hurry. We searched the rest of the house thoroughly, and then came back to the old man. He squirted us again, still laughing like a hyena." Owen chuckled lightly.

Pete chimed in, "All I could think was, where in hell did he get a little pink water pistol?"

Owen continued. "After we left and were back in the Humvee, Slingerland says, You guys smell like goat piss!"

"He squirted us with goat piss!" Pete said, with a belly laugh. Shelly laughed out loud and Bradley smiled slightly as he often did. Pete looked at Owen and cracked up again. It was as though a gate had been opened allowing pent up emotions to flow freely. Owen slapped Pete on the back and went for more beer. Shelly finished his beer and said he was giving it up for the night.

While Owen was gone, Bradley said, "Owen never talks about Afghanistan."

"None of us do," Pete said.

"His right hand trembles when he's confronted with tense situations," Bradley said.

Pete cupped his hand around his beer bottle and stared in. "We don't talk about it, so I'm asking you not to repeat me." Bradley nodded confirmation.

"We were on patrol checking houses for Taliban, just like we were doing when that old man squirted us with the water pistol. There were four of us on a narrow street with these little houses on each side. They're made of mud and sand, sort of like stucco, dark inside and out. They have flat roofs, and in the summertime the men sleep up there. You never know if it's an innocent citizen or someone waiting to ambush a patrol. One of the locals pointed out a house where he thought there was some suspicious activity, so we had to go in. When you're doing a raid, you go in locked and ready - clear the zone, and the next man follows you, single file. We had two guys in and I was right behind them. Owen was outside. It was dark and then the whole place was lit up with AK-47s, and I went down. I was hit right here," Pete pointed to the soft spot right above his shoulder blade. "It went right through me. It was never life threatening, but I was in shock. I'm thinking I'm gonna die, and then I hear that 16 rattling off twenty-five or thirty rounds, and then a hand under my armpit. It's Owen. He drags me outside and slams me against the wall. I've still got my 16 in my hand. Owen's headed back in. There's a guy on the roof with a .47, trying to get into position to take Owen out, but I sit up and put a round through him."

Pete hesitated, the expression on his face is dark and tense, struggling to get into the next phase of his story is painful.

"The house is so dark inside that it looks like lightning flashes and the sound is deafening. I don't see any way Owen comes out of there alive, so I'm up trying to get up and get back into the fight, but then Owen drags out our two guys. Cleve is gut shot, and he doesn't make it, and the other guy is Slingerland."

Pete stopped and gritted his teeth, fighting back tears. "The other guy is Slingerland, and now he's up there in the city on a Goddamn street corner begging for food." He stopped and sobbed quietly, finally giving into the feeling of dread he had been carrying around with him since seeing Slingerland in Birmingham.

"Owen's dragging Sling on his back and Sling is firing his 16 through the doorway when another one of our guys comes out of a Humvee and lights the place up with a M203 grenade launcher. I feel the flash on my face, and I know it's over. I scream, *die motherfuckers!*" Pete stopped, the memory was embedded in the lines on his face. "Owen's right hand was trembling. It was like that for two days before it stopped. I guess it still does when he gets in a tight spot."

Owen was standing quietly behind Pete with three Land Sharks in his hands. He placed them on the picnic table, put both hands on Pete's shoulder and said, "I love you, brother."

That was the end of the conversation.

Chapter Twenty

Lee Ford and Tyrese Jefferson were traveling southbound on I-95 through South Carolina. Tyrese was driving and Lee had the laptop open reviewing the case information. "Here's what we've got," Lee said, scrolling through the information on the screen. "Arthur Sweeney and the mob were both on the internet researching John Wilkes Booth's diary. That's crazy, but it's right here," Lee said, tapping his finger on the screen.

"Arthur Sweeney was assistant curator of a little museum so that's not unusual for him, but why in hell is the mob interested in that kind of stuff? Either way, they were both researching details about Booth's diary, and Edwin Stanton, Abraham Lincoln's Secretary of War. Sweeney is murdered in his home, by guess who," Lee said. "The D.C. cops have all the crime scene info, so we have to wait and see on that stuff."

"We're waiting on the computer, but I got a text from the district police detective this morning – they're releasing it. Tech is picking it up this morning to transfer to Quantico." Tyrese said.

Lee was already aware of that; shook his head in agreement. "Sweeney is murdered, presumably a hit but we don't know if it was gambling or something to do with all this stuff about

Booth. Anyway, he's dead. Now this is the peculiar thing about all this. His son is working with another guy down in the historic district tearing out stuff presumably for an overall renovation. They get attacked – nearly murdered, but nobody knows why."

"Maybe sonny was into them for gambling just like his old man, and they were going to take both of them out for good measure," Tyrese said.

"I don't think so. He has a computer, but it was inactive for at least a year. Just recently it was up again researching this stuff about Booth. That's something we got back this morning, but there was nothing indicating gambling"

Tyrese grimaced, "What the hell?"

"Anyway, Sweeney's son and this guy, Owen Black split, and end up in Bon Secour, Alabama. Black's hometown is Leesville, Kentucky. Black's wife still lives there and she reported a burglary on the same day we were getting pings from Leesville on a throwaway back to Sorrento's in Manhatton. In a few hours there was activity on the web regarding one Peter Findley, a war buddy of Owen Black's."

"Have we got a time-line on all this?" Tyrese asked.

"I've got a numerical log." Lee said.

"It's obvious the mob is tracking them down, but why?"

"Swag gets a traffic ticket in Gulf Shores, a town twenty minutes from Bon Secour, so more than likely they've found them." Lee said.

The evidence was solid, although circumstantial. The conclusion was evident that Arthur Sweeney was murdered by the mob, particularly, Robert Swag. In contrast, there wasn't anything corroborating that it happened because of illegal gambling. The existence of that point excluded the FBI from conducting an official investigation into the homicide of Arthur Sweeney. The law doesn't preclude them from following a logical trail involving murder, but they don't have any more jurisdiction than the average citizen without local involvement. In this case Lee and Tyrese were investigating illegal possession of cultural artifacts, a federal crime, which gave them considerable leverage despite the fact Wodetzki had given it to Lee as a form of punishment.

"We don't have enough evidence to arrest Swag on murder, but we know he did it," Tyrese said.

"We don't have the goods on him yet, but we can't ignore the fact he's stalking our suspects in the illegal possession of artifacts case," Lee said.

"So, we're going to throw our weight around in our big possession of artifacts investigation," Tyrese laughed. Lee laughed too. "Whatever works," he said.

"I've got a suspicion that computer is going to shed light on a lot of things. If we can hang anything on Swag and it's got something to do with intrastate gambling, we're in like Flinn," Lee said.

As the sun was setting, a swift breeze was coming in from the Gulf. For several day's clouds had hovered over the ocean in the evening but nothing had come ashore – appeared dangerous but merely a glorious light show on the horizon. Swag and his crew had ventured out on four dry runs, maneuvering from Stanley's Marina to points offshore near Shelly's pier. Every time they had been out the weather looked threatening, but nothing ever developed.

The clouds in the distance looked like huge orange pillows in the darkening sky as lightning streaks lit up the parking lot at Stanley's in flashes that turned night into day. It looked different to Sal, but Swag was ignoring the breeze, and the heightened smell of rain in the air. Swag handed Sal three sawed-off shotguns in flexible leather cases, and a .357 magnum Smith & Wesson. A large drop of rain hit Sal, stinging his skin. "Bobby, this weather looks serious to me." Sal said.

"That thunder might be a good thing, good cover when we pop these little shorties on them guys," Swag said.

"If we don't sink before we get there," Sal said. The wind was streaming across the dock, the little catamaran was rocking in the water with the waves popping on the hull. "A little water ain't gonna hurt us, Sal. That little hood will keep us from getting too wet." Swag said. "It's not the rain I'm worried about, it's the wind and waves that might sink us, Bobby, and I can't swim."

"I can't swim neither, but it ain't even stormin' yet, Sal. It'll be okay."

Sal handed the guns to Mario. Mario raised an eyebrow, rolled his eyes, and exhaled. The wind was steady, Mario's hair was fluttering in the wind. Frank was standing in the boat swaying and stumbling as it rocked in the waves. "It's getting rough out here, Bobby!" Just at that instant thunder roared overhead, the lightning flashes were eerie, like a black strobe light glistering in the blackness of night.

"We got a job to do," Swag said as he made his way down the ladder and stepped into the boat. Sal, and Mario followed him. Sal cranked up the engine and backed the boat away from the slip. He shoved it into forward and headed out into the bay. They were out about a hundred yards when the wind roared sending the boat sideways. The water had been choppy, but now it was churning as though a giant agitator had been placed in front of them; water was pouring in as the rain came down in torrents.

"This is bullshit, Bobby!" Sal shouted.

Mario piped in, "Bobby, I'm not dying out here in the ocean just because we need to murder a couple of guys!"

Swag bristled, leaning forward he glared at Mario with fire in his eyes. "What did you say!" Swag bellowed.

"I said I don't want to die out here just because we have to take out a couple of guys." Mario yelled, trying to be heard over the thunder and rumbling waves.

"That's not what you said, Mario! You said 'cause we need to murder some guys!" Swag growled. "Turn the sonofabitch around, Sal. Get back to the slip!"

It was a harrowing adventure but in a few moments the catamaran was back in the slip. The four men made their way through the downpour to the Cadillac. Swag left the parking lot, but soon he was stuck behind a parade of cars with hazard lights flashing through the curtain of rain. They were all wet to the bone. "I'm glad you changed your mind on that shit, boss," Mario said.

Swag's face was like a stone as he stared straight ahead, his breathing was deep, and just before he spoke a growl emitted from his throat. "Mario, shut your frickin' mouth!" The big cat barked.

"What the fuck, Bobby?" Mario said meekly.

"Don't you ever call me a murderer again, Mario! And if you think this is murder you can get back to Jersey and hang it up! This ain't murder. This is business!"

"Bobby, I, ahh," Mario stuttered.

"Shut it, Mario. Let me explain something to you. These guys we're going after, they offended the organization. They fucked with the family. This ain't murder. Murder is when you kill innocent people. Have you seen that black flag flying over that fish place where these guys are staying. Viet Nam veterans fly that flag. That old man was over there killin' people, just like we kill people who fuck with us." Swag said. He took a deep breath and exhaled.

"That was war, Bobby," Sal said. The lights from the other vehicle were still flashing, and a curtain of rain was still beating down on them. Swag wiped water from his face with his shirtsleeve. "Do you think he didn't kill some innocent people over there, and even them gooks fightin' against our people was fighting for their own country. They thought we was the one who was wrong."

"My brother was in Viet Nam, Bobby," Frank said.

"I ain't sayin' nothing wrong about your brother, Frankie, I'm just sayin' we're in a war just like they was. I remember when I was a little kid Jack Kennedy and Lyndon Johnson was saying that the Commies were taken over the world. They said it was the domino effect. IF Viet Nam was to fall to the Commies, the next country would fall, and then another until they took over the whole world, like dominos falling. That's the way it is for us. If we let some guy like Arthur Sweeney take us for ninety thousand dollars, then the next guy will do the same thing, and then another, like dominos, and then we won't have a family no more. Them guys got something that belongs to the family, and they offended our organization, so killin' them is like an act of war."

"I'm sorry, Bobby. I was shaken up out there on that little boat, and I misspoke. I know you're no murderer, Bobby," Mario said apologetically. "We're all in this together."

"We'll regroup and get them later," Swag said. He put the Caddy into gear and drove out around the parade of cars into the heavy rain.

The storm was over but rain was still falling at a steady pace. Lightning flashes over the horizon and distant thunder were fading into the night. Pete and Owen were picking up debris that had blown in from the weeds and parking lot. Bradley was at the picnic table wearing a strange expression, reading a text on his I-phone. He had been in contact with Luther Goodall, a friend of his mother's, a lawyer who practiced in Virginia. The information he was receiving was both exciting and nerve-racking at the same time

Pete stuffed the junk he had collected into the trash can, dusted off his hands and sat down beside Bradley. "What's this worried look I see on you face?"

Bradley was quiet for a long time before speaking. "I've done something that might make you guys a little mad," he said.

Owen dropped his debris and walked to the table to join the other two. "What's that, Bradley?"

"I've been appointed to be Carl Slingerland's guardian."

Both Pete and Owen were jolted by the remark. "What do you mean?" Owen asked.

"I'm Slingerland's guardian." Bradley said

"I don't get it. What do you mean?" Owen asked again.

"I don't know much about the law, but don't you need a court order for something like that?" Pete asked, completely perplexed.

"I've got a court order."

"You've got a court order?" Owen asked, even more astonished than Pete had been. He took a seat across from Bradley on the picnic table. "I guess I don't understand," he said. "Maybe you could explain."

"I have a lawyer in Virginia – a pretty high-profile lawyer. He was a friend of my mothers, and he told her before she died that if I ever needed anything, I could call on him. I've never needed anything before, but now I want to help Slingerland, so I sent a text to him. He called me and I explained the situation. He went to work on it and was able to get me appointed as Slingerland's Guardian, and we have a rehabilitation and counseling center in Fulton where he will be admitted under a different court order. I just need to get him into Baldwin County to have him committed."

"That takes money," Owen said, still somewhat overwhelmed.

"How in hell did you accomplish that?" Pete said.

"Luther said Baldwin County was the most corrupt county in Alabama, and if you have enough money you can get anything you want here," Bradley said.

"Luther who?" Owen asked.

"Luther Goodall."

"Holy moly! The Luther Goodall who won all those cigarette lawsuits, and now he's on those mesothelioma cases?" Pete asked.

"Yes."

"How much is this going to cost, Bradley?"

"It's all paid for, Owen. I just need to get him back to Baldwin County. Luther said law enforcement outside of this county would be reluctant to help, but if we -well, if I get him here, they have to help or be held in contempt of court."

There was an agitated expression on Pete's face. His eyebrows were furrowed, his lips in a tight line. "Bradley, you keep saying I - that I'm going to get him back to Baldwin County." Pete said, emphasizing the I. "What's that shit all about? Why would you exclude Owen and me on something like that?"

"I didn't want to presume anything. I didn't want to put anything on you guys. I just hope you're not ticked off."

"I've been worried about that sonofabitch since I saw him in Birmingham. There's no way you're going up there without me," Pete said. Owen was studying Bradley's face. He imagined he knew Bradley better than anyone. They had spent every waking moment together since that awkward meeting in their tiny little apartment back in D.C., but this surprised him. "Bradley, why didn't you say something about this. What were you thinking?"

"Owen, I've never done anything for anyone in my life, I've just survived and tried to stay out of the way. I'm learning from you that things matter. You work hard and sacrifice to send money home to your wife, even after she broke your heart. You were kind to me when I didn't think there was any kindness left in the world. You fought to save our lives. You never lecture or express your opinions, but you show me by example that things matter. This thing with Slingerland matters."

"That's more words than I've heard you say since we met. I guess I have to be all in on this, and you're right, Slingerland matters." Owen said.

Chapter Twenty-One

After Shelly was updated on the plan to rescue Slingerland, he was immediately ready to help put things into motion. The 150 didn't have enough passenger area to transport four grown men, so Shelly volunteered to drive his 1985 Ford Station wagon. It was brown with woodgrain panels on the doors, whitewall tires and a luggage rack on top. Smoke billowed out of the tailpipe for a short time after it was started, but after settling down it purred like a kitten. It was big, plenty big enough for the four of them. And if everything went as planned, sufficient to carry Slingerland back to Baldwin County. It was a mere 275 miles from Bon Secour to Birmingham, but Shelly threw a couple of quarts of 10w30 oil into the cargo area for good measure.

Carl Slingerland was on the corner of 13th and Wallace. He was dressed in oil-stained coveralls, hair with several holes exposing his pale skin, unkept hair and wonting of personal hygiene. A shopping cart was parked on the curb filled with blankets, and coffee cans full of scraps procured from dumpsters in allies behind local restaurants. A beard full of crud and a scab on his cheek left him a pitiful caricature of the man he had been.

Each time traffic stopped at the signal Carl paced alongside the street holding a cardboard sign stating that he was a disabled homeless vet. When the light changed he would hit the walk button to hasten the time between stops. Carl had a slight limp caused by the bullet he took in Afghanistan on the occasion when Owen drug him to safety. Most people passing by thought he was faking it, some thought he was faking it but gave him a money anyway. As he took the money he would say, "God bless you."

Carl took in between thirty and forty dollars per day. It was enough to buy whiskey, and food from McDonalds. It might have bought a single room in a scruffy old rooming house downtown but purchasing a fifth of hard liquor took a hefty bite out of his profits. When he had money left over he fed some of the others who were living beneath the overpass on I-24. Carl was 38 years old but he looked like he was seventy.

A City of Birmingham utility truck was making its way up Wallace Street. Men in green vests were stringing Christmas lights as a light mist permeated the air. It was cold and miserable. Red and blue flashing lights behind the utility truck from a Birmingham Police cruiser protected the workers from traffic as they went about their duties.

Shelly was nervous driving up 13th St., signaling with an outstretched arm indicating a left turn onto Wallace Street. Pete and Owen laughed each time he manually rolled down the window and stuck his arm out into the wind. Bradley was busy taking in the scenery.

Slingerland was slouched beneath a huge black broken umbrella, one side hanging like a black bird with a broken wing. Owen and Pete were stretching their necks to take a look at him, not confident that it was their old friend tucked under that frayed fabric.

Finally, Pete said, "That's him."

Owen wasn't so sure. This was the first time he had seen him since he drug him out of that house in Afghanistan with his leg full of hot lead. Slingerland was hustled off the battlefield to the combat support hospital. He was treated and discharged soon thereafter. Owen tried to find him but it was like he had dropped off the face of the earth. Now he knew where he had gone.

Shelly lowered his arm out the window and pulled over to the curb. The utility truck with the workers installing the Christmas lights rolled up the street a little closer. Flashing red and blue lights glistened in the mist as the squad car followed behind it.

As Owen, Pete, Bradley and Shelly approached, Slingerland tilted the umbrella back to take a look at them. "I'm a homeless disabled veteran. I could use some help," he said. His eyes met Owen's gaze. In a moment of recognition, his eyebrows raised, and then immediately he looked at the ground.

"Help a guy out," he said, avoiding further eye contact. Pete squatted on his haunches to peer under the umbrella. "Sling, it's Owen and me."

"Mister, a few bucks would help, I'm hungry," he said,

"It's me, Sling. We're here to help."

"I don't need your fucking help, Pete! I'm trying to make a living here. Leave me alone."

Owen kneeled down, "Sling, we're going to take you to a place where they can help you."

"Owen, I don't need help. You fuckers need to get out of here!" He jumped up with surprising quickness. The umbrella rolled off the sidewalk into the street. Bradley hurried to retrieve it. Shelly watched, studying every move he made. Slingerland picked up his cardboard sign and waved it in the air. "Help me out here!" He shouted.

Just at that moment another disheveled man with his own sign approached them. "Could you spare a little change. I'm stranded, brother."

"He's a fucking imposter, man!" Slingerland shouted. "A guy drops him off here every morning. There are others too, some of them down on 12th Street. They're frauds!"

Pete took Slingerland's elbow. "Sling, we need to get off the street." Slingerland jerked his arm away, stumbling backwards nearly falling. Pete hurried to catch him. A police siren cut through the air as the squad car that had been blocking for the utility truck accelerated to the curb and skidded to a stop. A large policeman got out of the squad car and approached them. "What's going on here," he demanded.

"He's a friend," Owen said.

"It looks like a fight to me," the officer said.

Owen explained the situation as Slingerland listened, pacing up and down the sidewalk. The cop had a disinterested expression, occasionally glancing across the street to check the progress of the utility crew. Owen was still talking when the officer interrupted. "I can't get the sonofabitch off the street. The Supreme Court ruled it's a free speech issue. I don't care what you do with the worthless bastard, but if you get him off my street --"

Shelly charged between Owen and the cop, "Hey! Keep a civil tongue in your mouth! This man is a Navy Seal. He's a war hero!" he barked. It became suddenly quiet. Slingerland stared at Shelly with a fragile glimmer in his eyes, and then they filled with tears. Owen walked over and put his arms around him. Slingerland buried his face in Owen's shoulder and cried. The cop walked away.

Slingerland fretted about his things. He wondered what might happen to his grocery cart, and his spot beneath I-24, but he slid into the back seat of Shelly's car, and got the details regarding Bradley's guardianship, and the rehabilitation center in Fulton. It was as though he had been waiting for redemption, and it had finally come. His resistance came from resentment, and a sense of abandonment, but the alienation he had endured was fading.

The smell in the back seat was overwhelming even with the windows down. Shelly was the first to suggest that they get a suite in a Holiday Inn to allow Slingerland the opportunity to "freshen up." As they drove through Birmingham, Slingerland seemed more coherent – not so agitated and defensive. "I don't want to blame anyone for my situation, but you guys abandoned me," he said quietly." His breath was terrible, his condition deplorable and in any situation it would have been easy to take anything he said with a grain of salt, but Pete and Owen knew him. They knew there was substance in his character that somehow had been stripped from him.

"We didn't abandon you, Sling, you were discharged. We thought you went home," Owen said.

"I never had a home before I went into the military, Afghanistan was my home. Seal Team Six was my family. When I came back to the States I could never get anything right. I didn't fit in."

"We all had a hard time getting back to civilian life, Sling. We were all effected by what happened over there. I still think about it," Pete said.

It was strange to be talking to Slingerland in a rational manner. His appearance and apparent lack of mental and psychological clarity notwithstanding, yet they were talking as though it didn't matter. Owen almost felt totally removed from reality.

"I'm not on drugs," Slingerland said quietly. Nobody commented. "I drink a fifth of whiskey every day, but I'm not on drugs." He waited for a long moment before starting again. "Owen, you told me several times that during hell week you wanted to check out – to quit, but you couldn't walk out in front of the other guys and ring that bell, to turn your insides out and show the world who you really were. You didn't think you were strong enough or good enough, but in the end, you were, and more. You had more grit inside than the rest of us."

Owen was quiet, Slingerland was right about hell week. He wouldn't have made it through without fearing the disgrace of walking out in front of the team to ring the bell announcing his defeat. In battle it was the same thing, he didn't think he could do it, he was weak and afraid but he did things he didn't think he could do and it was only because he didn't want to let others down. If he had been alone out there, he would have run.

"That's what happened to me" Slingerland said. "I wanted to keep going, but you guys didn't bother to contact me, or to let me know you still cared about me. I was important out there in the field, I was strong and invincible, I was part of something bigger than me, and then I was nothing. I didn't matter anymore. There wasn't anyone here to keep me from ringing that bell. I've been ringing it every day since then," he said. He tightened his lip and bit back tears.

Shelly drove into the Holiday Inn parking lot. He stopped the car, got out and opened the back door. Slingerland shakily stepped out. Shelly put his hands on his shoulders, looked Slingerland straight into his eyes. "Your matter, Carl. When you get out of the rehab center, you're going to work for me. We're going to be your family, but brother, you stink. We have to get you cleaned up."

Slingerland smiled.

The sound of bacon crackling on the gridle; the aroma was permeating the air in the house as Swag worked methodically over the kitchen range, turning eggs with the skill of a practiced cook. Mario was first to join Swag, and the other two were soon to follow. "I didn't know you could work that kind of magic over a stove, Bobby," Mario said.

"I worked in the kitchen at Carmine's down on Seventh Street while I was working my way up in the organization. It was the best job I ever had. That's how I got this," he said, patting his stomach. He slid two eggs, over easy, onto a plate, added three bacon strips and handed it to Mario. He followed suit with Sal and Frank.

"You guys eat, I already had mine before you got outta bed."

Sal crunched a piece of bacon and toast, and sipped coffee before he spoke, "What's the plan for the day, Bobby?"

Swag wiped his hands with a towel, picked up his coffee cup and sipped. "Well, we got to get this job done tonight if there ain't no more hurricanes. You guys want to see the beach, so I guess you can do that if you want to. I thought I'd look around a little."

"Having a few drinks, Bobby?" Mario asked.

"Some, but not too much. I don't want nothin' cloudin' my thinkin'. We need to get this job done." There was a little angst in his tone.

"Bobby, none of us are rookies here. I've been in this for seven years, and Mario's been in since he was a kid. John Gotti was fucking things up when he was coming up. Franky's the only one here who's new at this." Sal said.

"Yeah, but this ain't the same as up in Philly, or down in the Bronx. We don't know nothing about the land, or the streets, or how the cops operate around here. Up there we know things, we know the businesses, and we got cops watching our backs. I ain't never done a job without a cop around the corner keeping an eye out for me. Down here we got nothin'."

"I guess you're right, Bobby, but sometimes I think you got no faith in the rest of us."

"Better safe than sorry, Sal. Better safe than sorry."

After breakfast Swag was good to his word. He loaded his crew into the Caddy and drove to the corner of Route 59 and East Beach Boulevard. The Hang Out Restaurant and bar was on one corner, The Pink Pony on the other. They were sitting within a stone's throw from the Gulf of Mexico, with white sand and beach umbrellas, but one was an upscale tourist destination, and the other a hold-over from the fifties. The Pink Pony was just as its name indicated. It was pink stucco, with a deck facing the beach, and a flat roof supporting air conditioners and exhaust vents. It stuck out like a sore thumb, an eyesore that had survived the building boom the Alabama gulf coast had enjoyed for the last thirty years. Minus the deck, the sand and the ocean, The Pink Pony would have fit in on a side street in East St. Louis, Illinois. As awful as it was the place was generally packed with customers. There wasn't a place on the beach that was more appealing to Swag than The Pink Pony. Swag parked the car in an overflow parking area across the street from The Hang Out, and the four of them walked to The Pink Pony. Sal, Mario, and Frank, dressed in their colorful beach shirts, baggy shorts and bright white gym shoes, walked out onto the beach. Swag went to the deck of The Pink Pony. He sat near the railing and sipped on a glass of Pinot Noir.

Lee Ford and Tyrese Jefferson had just checked into the Phoenix All Suites condominium overlooking the beach. It was an old place, one of the first high-rise condos in Gulf Shores, but because of strict maintenance and management it was still a quality place to stay. In each condo there were two bedrooms, a kitchen and a living room. Every unit faced the beach, with a balcony and a clear view of the ocean. The only drawback was the ugly little pink bar and grill setting right beneath it. Even though the deck was on the far side jutting out into the sand, residents in the Phoenix could see it clearly.

Lee unpacked his bag, checked the refrigerator and popped a Bud light. There were strict rules in the FBI about drinking on duty, but although it was still in the mid-afternoon the only official function Lee had was to review the evidence and discuss it with Tyrese. It was sixty-four degrees; a nice breeze flowing in from the Gulf. Lee walked out onto the balcony to take a look at the surroundings. Lee was surprised when he saw The Pink Pony - that little blot on the landscape. All the other upscale condos, and the newly constructed Hang Out, with a restaurant, bar, and elevated stages for concerts made it look even more homely.

Lee sipped his beer and scanned the activity in the sand below. It was cool but the beach was full of girls and women in bikinis and guys in swimming suits. Tyrese stepped through the sliding glass door with his cell phone in his hand. "Shelly Barnett's license plate number was run early this afternoon in Birmingham."

"Shelly Barnett, the Shelly Barnett who owns Shelly's Seafood Company?"

"The one and only."

"Do we know why?"

"The best I can tell is that he was obstructing traffic and was issued a verbal warning."

"Strange," Lee said.

Lee turned his bottle up and finished his Bud Light. When he sat the empty on the rail he straightened up with a jolt. "What the hell!" he gasped.

"What's wrong," Tyrese asked.

"Do you see that big guy on the deck of that Pink joint down there?"

"The fat guy by the railing?"

"Yep, that's Bobby Swag. Do you believe that shit!"

"What now?" Tyrese asked.

Lee went back into the condo and opened his briefcase where two nine-millimeter Smith and Wessons were neatly packed beside a variety of gadgets he kept on hand that were issued by the Bureau. He picked out a credit card sized GPS tracker. The flat dark plastic card was small enough to fit easily into a wallet, it was magnetized, and contained a series of digits.

"I don't usually handle this end of thnigs, but the tech guys gave me a couple of these just in case I found myself in a situation like this," he said. "These things don't even exist as far as the public's concerned.

"We used them at Quantico in our training. My cell phone and computer are compatible, all we need to do is program it in and the computer does the work," Tyrese said. For the moment both Lee and Tyrese had forgotten about Swag sitting on the deck at The Pink Pony, both so impressed with their new top of the line GPS tracker that the importance of the moment had escaped them. "You probably had these in use when your guy skipped the country, huh?" Lee glanced at Tyrese and chuckled. Tyrese was smiling.

In a few moments Lee and Tyrese were in the parking lot looking for Swag's Cadillac. Lee had several pictures of the car on his cell phone and the license number from the ticket he got for ignoring the pedestrian crosswalk. It wasn't much of a task to find the big boat in the parking lot. Tyrese was on his knees placing the tracker on the Caddy's frame when an old guy dressed in plaid knee-length shorts, a baggy long-sleeved yellow shirt and glasses so thick his eyes were floating around like two boiled eggs in a glass of water. He shuffled up to Tyrese and poked him with his cane. Tyrese jumped out of his skin.

"What are you doing to my car, boy!"

Tyrese scrambled to his feet. Lee had been watching The Pink Pony parking lot for Swag but diverted his attention to the new dilemma. He hurried to join Tyrese. The old man was waving his cane in the air, stumbling, and mumbling obscenities. Tyrese had a look of horror on his face. Lee stepped between them. "It's okay, Mister. Nothing going on here," Lee said.

"The hell there ain't. This boy here is trying to steal my car!"

Tyrese put his hand on the old man's arm, "It's okay, man. I'm not feeling well, I was just catching my breath," he said.

"Get your Godamned dirty hands off me!" the old man said, jerking his arm away, stumbling backwards, heading for the ground. Lee grabbed him just inches before he hit the dirt. Lee was cranking his neck to be sure Swag wasn't coming into view as he put the old boy back on his feet.

A little old woman dressed in a white long-sleeved blouse and coral colored slacks, wearing a wide brim beach bonnet approached them. "That's not your car, Herman," she said, curtly. Herman turned and looked at her, totally disoriented.

"What!"

"Your car's in the other parking lot. Remember, Cody drove us down here in your car. It's over there."

"This is my car! He's trying to steal it!"

A twenty something young man hurried up to join them. "Grandpa, this is not your car. This isn't even the same kind of car as yours," he said. He took grandpa by his elbow and turned him around. "See your car is over there."

"This isn't my car?" he asked, still irritated.

"No, this isn't your car. Your car is over there," he said. At that point Cody and his grandmother each took and arm and guided grandpa towards the other parking lot. He was stiff legged, jerking his cane around carelessly in the air as he went. After a ten feet trek, the old guy turned feebly around, glared at Tyrese and said, "You sonofabitch!"

Lee laughed. Tyrese shot him a dirty look. "I got it. We need to get out of here."

Robert Swag was still on the Pink Pony deck half way through his second bottle of pinot noir, His associates were still out on the beach watching women in their bathing suits.

Lee and Tyrese were back in the condo. Tyrese was loading the computer program for the GPS tracker. He was quietly mulling over the incident with the confused senior citizen. His features conveyed an emotion between irritation and curiosity. Lee was reviewing the federal statutes regarding illegal possession of cultural artifacts.

"Tyrese, did you know that a woman gave President Clinton a hat she had made with an eagle feather in it, and she was arrested for possessing feathers from an endangered species?"

"Yes," Tyrese said still irritated.

"That's crazy, huh?" Lee asked.

Tyrese was quiet for a long moment before he spoke. "Lee, explain to me how being called the most derogatory name in the history of mankind is funny? I expect these old bigots here in the south to talk like that but I didn't think my partner was so insensitive he would laugh about it."

"I know you're upset, but if you'll give me a minute to think about it, I'll try," Lee said. "I'll wait," Tyrese said, leaning forward with his hands hanging between his knees.

"I don't think being called derogatory names or racial slurs, is funny. That old guy – what he said was completely idiotic. It made me laugh." Lee said. He paused trying to gather his thoughts. He cleared his throat nervously and began again. "I'm going to tell you an off-color joke. Before you get mad or judgmental, allow me to finish."

"A joke?"

"Yes, it goes like this. A black man was found dead in a river wrapped in chains down in Mississippi. When they drug him out of the water the Sheriff said, it was just like that boy to steal more chain than he could swim across the river with."

Tyrese bolted up straight. "You think that's a joke?"

"Let me put it into context. Now, when people laugh at that joke it's because it points out the absurdity of racism. It's only funny because nobody in the world would think like that. It's the absurdity they're laughing at. They laugh because way down inside they're happy that it's not them. It elevates them to a higher level. They laugh because the absurdity of that kind of deduction is proof that they are better than someone who thinks like that, and they have the ability to recognize it. They're smarter than that guy, and better. It feels so good to be better than someone else you have to laugh. It's the same thing when you see someone fall. You're not really happy that someone fell on their ass in front of a bunch of people. You laugh because you're happy down deep inside in that place where you have that laugh reflex tucked away that it wasn't you."

Tyrese scratched his head and laughed. "Man, you are full of shit," he said.

"I'm sorry I laughed when that old geezer called you those names." Lee said. There was a slight smile beginning to form as he watched Tyrese for his reaction. Tyrese smiled and turned back to his computer.

Shelly insisted on footing for a suite at the Holiday Inn, but Owen objected vehemently. Despite everything he had been through, Owen still believed in paying your own way. The expression "being a man" still had meaning to him. Slingerland was his friend and it was his obligation to pay the bill. He stuck with Shelly like glue as they approached the desk knowing the generous old buzzard would fork out the dough for the suite if he wasn't there to put a claim on it. They were both surprised to find the bill had already been paid including any amenities accumulated during their stay. They questioned the clerk, but she could only say that it was someone anonymous. Owen was enwrapped by an uneasy feeling as they made their way to the suite. Pete was just as curious about this "Mana from heaven." There was certainly something going on beneath the surface in a place where they couldn't see. Was there a Miss Haversham or an elusive criminal behind the curtain pulling the strings or a distant relative buying redemption for his sins? It didn't feel right but Owen assuaged his innate warning and continued to the suite. They were even more puzzled when they opened the door to find it was expansive, almost luxurious. Owen was surprised that Holiday Inn had suites at this level. It had a kitchenette, two bedrooms with two queens each, and a generous lounging area. If Slingerland had ever been in such an elaborate accommodation he had forgotten. His eyes opened in astonishment and brightened to take it all in. Just as quickly there was a moment of recognition, he stiffened and tried to back out. Pete put his arm around him and said, "It's alright, buddy, you earned this." Shelly said, "You're with family now."

As the sun was setting Birmingham, Slingerland was standing in the warm shower water as it cascaded through his hair and off his shoulder. A brown stream made its way across the tub and into the drain. He leaned his head into the wall. Grateful tears filled his eyes and he said, "Thank you, God."

Back in Bon Secour Swag parked the Caddy, popped the trunk and divvyed out cases containing guns and ammunition. As they walked across the pier at Stanley's Marina, long shadows were cast across the deck as the setting sun was sinking below the horizon. The sky a deep blue with huge round white clouds, orange and red glowing like a fire behind them.

"Red sky at night, sailor's delight," Mario said cheerfully.

"What's the supposes to mean?" Swag said impatiently.

"It means no hurricanes tonight," Mario said.

"Oh, that's good, Mario. I'm glad you're the fuckin' weatherman now." Swag was losing his patience with Mario. Even though Mario was annoying to everyone, it wore on Swag more than anyone else.

"Mario, I heard one time that Billy the Kid shot a man 'cause he was snoring too loud. Snoring got under his skin like when people say stupid shit all the time."

"Did you read that somewhere, Bobby?"

"I said I heard it, Mario!" Swag growled.

Swag planted a .38 snub-nose in Mario's hand and shoved it into his gut. "Take this and put in your belt. "Don't say nothin' else until I ask you something," Swag said. Mario flinched, backed up and said cheerfully, "You got it, Bobby."

The trip from Stanley's Marina to Shelly's pier was uneventful. The water was like silk glimmering from the moonlight in the eastern sky. The hum from the little catamaran was quiet, katydids and crickets on shore were clamoring in the darkness. It was as peaceful as a Sunday morning prayer meeting. Everything was dark at Shelly's Seafood Company. Swag hadn't counted on the full moon lighting up the parking lot so brightly. If he was doing this job alone he would have scrapped it for a better day. Carlos had assigned Sal, Mario and Frank to assist him, and when the boss made decisions Swag wasn't about to protest. Still if he had his druthers, he would be in that little boat alone. Carlos wasn't all that interested the seventeen missing pages

Arthur Sweeney vowed had enormous value, but Swag wanted them more now than ever. It was redemption for him.

Swag was fearless, but he was careful. He didn't want to run into a bullet. He would never backing down, but he wasn't going to fail because he had been sloppy. He didn't trust Sal, Mario or Frank. They were sloppy, and they didn't have the loyalty to the family he had.

Swag went first as they ascended the ladder onto Shelly's pier. He grunted as he raised his leg and hoisted himself onto the dock. "This place is dark as a graveyard," he said.

"It's a full moon, Bobby," Mario said.

"I'm talkin' about the fish place, Mario. I don't remember asking you a question neither," Swag said, glaring at Mario.

"The place where they're staying is over there in that brush. There's an old trailer and an open air shed," Sal said.

"How do you know that?" Swag asked curtly.

"I got pictures from Vinney he got off Google Earth." Sal said. "From the computer?" Swag asked.

"Yes. I'll take the lead, Bobby. That's where they're staying." Swag frowned and followed Sal. In the moonlight they were as washed out as four phantom figures materializing from the grave. One single dangling bulb was visible shining in the pavilion. Sal crept slowly down the path in the weeds with the double barrel shotgun cocked and ready. Swag was right behind him with the other two in single file behind him. A breeze was rocking the hammock, the palm trees rasping as air flowed through the palms, but it was as quiet as death. Swag walked to the trailer door motioning for Frank to join him. "Kick it," he whispered. A swift well-placed boot on the hinges sent the door open wildly. Swag rushed through the trailer with his shotgun leading the way, knocking furniture over like a mad bull. He didn't stop until he reached the far wall. The trailer was empty. When Swag returned to the outside the other three were waiting.

"They're not here, Bobby," Mario said.

"No shit, Mario. They're not here. We need to put everything back the way we found it. You go back in the weeds and watch for them just in case they come back."

"There's snakes in the weeds, Bobby."

"There's a hella of lot worse out here than a snake if ya don't do what I tell ya," Swag said. Mario moved cautiously down the path and into the weeds. If they come back let 'em come on in. Yell to us and then start shootin'. We'll do our part on this end,"

Swag, Sal and Frank searched every crevasse in the pavilion and trailer but came up empty. They put everything back where they found it. Owen's truck was sitting in Shelly's lot with the doors unlocked. The seventeen pieces of paper were there in open view behind the driver's seat. Swag walked right past it on their way in and again on their way back to the boat. They sailed away into the night with no more accomplished than when they came in.

Back at the house Swag stopped Sal in the driveway. He glared at Sal for a long time before speaking. Sal paced nervously.

"Sal, get you bags and get the fuck outta here," Swag growled.

"What the fuck, Bobby. What's your problem?" Sal said angrily.

"Where'd you get them pictures of that place?"

"I told you Vinney got 'em from Goggle Earth. You gotta agree they were helpful."

"How'd you get 'em Sal?"

"Vinney sent them to my cell phone. I just looked at 'em and turned the phone off.

"Sal, be gone by morning," Swag said as he walked away.

The distinctive sound of traffic on I-24 mingled with the steady trickling of rain on the parking lot asphalt. Shelly was standing beneath the canopy watching the cars and trucks casting a mist into the cool December air. His mind traversing time, his thoughts gathering to the time when he was on the tarmac at the airport in Oakland, California. He was already worn out from the long trip, a loss of essence meandering around in his brain, leaving him empty and alone. Shelly was drafted into the army so he went. Many of his friends demonstrated against the war in Viet Nam, but he never considered anything like that. It was hard leaving civilian life, but he was finding it harder to return. Every ounce of his being had been left in the jungle on that battlefield. One week before shipping out he was wading through a shallow muddy tributary to the Yellow River with his M-16 held high over his head scanning the riverbank and the treeline waiting for bullets to rain down on him and his buddies. He needed all his senses on alert to stay alive. It consumed him. Now as he walked across the airstrip with his duffle bag slung over his shoulder there was a small gathering of college students beyond the fence carrying signs that said, "Baby killer", and "End the war now." A long haired twenty something man hurled a horse turd at him. Shelly gritted his teeth remembering the flag-covered caskets that had made the trip with him, lined up behind the cargo plane as horse shit was flying across the runway. A blast from the horn of a semi-truck on I-24 shocked him back the present. Shelly grimaced and whispered, "Father, forgive them, they know not what they do."

Owen was awakened at 6:45 a.m. That was late for him. Pete was up hurriedly dressing. Shelly, Bradley and Slingerland gone. They both rushed down the stairs in lieu of taking the elevator. Bradley was sitting on a chair in front of the fireplace. When he saw Owen and Pete he pointed outside to the canopy. Pete was first to get through the sliding glass door. "Shelly, where's Sling?" he asked excitedly. Shelly pointed, "He's out there under the overpass. He had the shakes this morning. I came down with him. That's where he wanted to be." Shelly paused for a very long moment. "I get it, Pete." Owen and Pete got it too.

The trip from Birmingham was quiet. When they checked Slingerland into rehab, they said everything was already processed. Owen wondered if it was done by the New York lawyer or had someone worked their magic again anonymously. Slingerland was ready. He knew he had hit rock bottom. He was thankful he had been rescued. Owen, Bradley and Pete all hugged him, but when Shelly said so long, tears welled in Slingerland's eyes. "When you're out of here, you have a home, a job, and us guys too if you want us," Shelly said. On their way back from the rehab center conversation was short and sweet. They were all within their own thoughts. As they were driving into the parking lot Bradley said, "Chloe's coming."

Owen looked a little shocked. "Chloe's coming here?"

"Yes, Chloe's coming here."

"Okay," Owen said.

Chapter Twenty-Two

Lee Ford and Tyrese Jefferson followed the tracker they had attached to Swag's Caddy. When Swag and his crew took to the sea Lee knew in a short time they were enroute to Shelly's Seafood Company. He and Tyrese raced to Shelly's ahead of them, made a cursory search and determined nobody was there. They watched from the entrance as Swag and the others ascended the ladder from the slip to the pier and crossed the parking lot. The trailer and pavilion were too far back in the brush and trees to see what they were doing, but Tyrese videoed everything else. When they were back at the Phoenix they enhanced the video, ran it through face recognition and identified all four wise guys. Swag, they already knew, and now they had identification on the others.

Before the trip to Birmingham to extract Slingerland from the streets, Bradley called Warburton's Bar and Grill and contacted Chloe. Although there was never a stated interest between them, it was always there. It was flowing from Chloe like a bright light whenever they were together. Bradley was working a menial job and his future wasn't exactly blooming into anything meaningful. He was working in a wholesale seafood company peeling shrimp. Chloe had a Bachelor's Degree in social science, a degree worth literally nothing in the work force. She owed a hundred thousand dollars in student loans, and she was a waitress in a bar. But still, Chloe was an optimist and there was something irresistible about Bradley, so she was willing to take a chance. She worried and fretted about his sudden departure, hoping every day he would walk through the door at Warburton's. When he called she was almost speechless. After a brief conversation he said, "I miss you."

"Where are you, Bradley?

"Bon Secour, Alabama. It's near Gulf Shores," he said.

"I've got vacation time. I'm coming," she said. The phone went silent, and Bradley smiled.

The lights were turned down low in the condo. Lee's face was glowing in the light of the computer. "This Mario dude has been in organized crime since the eighties, Sal for about eight or ten years, but this Frank guy is new. He might be vulnerable when the heat's turned up," Lee said.

Tyrese seemed disinterested; he already knew the vague background details on all four suspects, but his cell phone was pinging, alerting him to an update. "Hey, Lee, Sal rented a car from Enterprise this morning. What do you think about that?

"Humm, I don't know. Swag always uses his old Caddy, and from everything we know about him that Caddy is exclusive transportation, no matter what," Lee said rubbing his chin.

"You know those guys were on their way to murder those guys last night, don't you," Tyrese said.

"Yep, they sure were, but we can't prove that." Lee said. He thought for a long moment and then slammed the laptop shut. "If those dicks in D.C. could make a little progress on the home invasion, we could actually make a move on this!" His voice raised in frustration. "What about the computer we sent to Quantico? Any news on that?"

"They're backed up, Lee. They have a mountain of crap ahead of us. This isn't national security. As far as they're concerned we're working on an Illegal Possession of Cultural Artifacts case," Tyrese said.

I guess we'll have to update the local Sheriff on this. I don't know how much help they'll be but we can't let these guys be murdered. We gotta alert the locals." Lee said.

"Today?"

"Yes, sometime today."

Bradley and Chloe had texted back and forth for two days as Chloe made her way from D.C. to Gulf Shores. She checked in at the Phoenix Suites at 6:30 a.m. The multi-story condos were shadows in the dark dotted with a yellow glow from windows on several levels. A garbage truck was growling in The Hang Out parking lot, the waves were pounding on the beach. Excitement and anticipation and apprehension advanced upon her like the surf crashing onto shore. Chloe had been to Virginia Beach, and Fort Lauderdale on spring break, but this was the first time she had come this far on her own. It was scary, but it felt good down deep inside in an unknown location, a place where she had never been and could not describe.

Bradley was nervous. He had cleared it with Shelly for a day off. Shelly looked at him like a proud grandfather and asked him if he needed a little extra dough. Bradley bashfully refused. He took a cab even after Owen offered the F150. Owen seemed a little hurt when he refused.

Chloe threw her arms around Bradley and kissed him. He was surprised. He kissed her back, fearing she would laugh, apologize and run for her car, disappointed and embarrassed. She wasn't though. She held onto him for a long time looking at him as though she had never seen anything so beautiful. A lot of things would happen in Bradley's life, but he would never forget that moment.

Chloe was dressed in a two-piece mustard colored swimming suit and a lightweight white coverup. Bradley was wearing blue jeans and a royal blue polo. Both were new and fit perfectly, but not suitable for the beach. Chloe invited him up to her suite. She had purchased a swimming suit and a Salt Life t-shirt, knowing he wouldn't have proper gear for walking in the sand and water.

They sat on the deck at The Pink Pony, both having coffee as the sun crept up peeking between the condos behind them, casting a line on the sea, glittering on the horizon. Small talk was easy – books, music and movies were all fodder for conversation. Chloe was amazed at all that Bradley had read. When she said as much, he responded, "I read Of Mice And Men four times in six weeks." Chloe laughed.

"It was the only book I had left when I left when I went to D.C.," he said quietly. The memory of being with Arthur in Charlottesville lingered in the back of his mind.

"I never read it. It was on our required reading list in high school. All the boys read it because it was so short, but the girls read other stuff. What's it about?"

"It was sad. It was about two men who were traveling together. One of them was mentally challenged, innocent, but prone to get into trouble. It had a terrible ending."

"But you read it four times in six weeks?" Chloe smiled.

"I kind of related to it. I was the dumb guy and Owen was the other guy," he said. Chloe laughed. "You're smart! You're shy but you're really smart."

"They traveled together, and the smart guy took care of the other one. Owen doesn't take care of me, but he looks out for me. He's given me a better outlook on life."

They walked on the beach as the sun inched higher in the sky. Chloe shed her coverup. Her long brown hair fluttered in the breeze as the tide rolled in wave upon wave. Her large brown eyes fixed on Bradley so much that she didn't see every man on the beach, young and old, gawking at her with admiration. Chloe was chatty about everything, but she kept coming back to Bradley's relationship with Owen. Finally, she said, "Bradley, I like you a lot, so I have to ask you this," she hesitated, then nervously asked, "Are you gay?"

In his quiet and usual manor, Bradley smiled. Chloe giggled because she knew it was an inappropriate question but there was a little strained expression on her face. She waited for what seemed forever. Finally, Bradley said, "No, I'm not gay. Neither is Owen, he just means a lot to me. We travel together like George and Lennie in Of Mice and Men. We take care of each other."

Talking more than he ever did in his life, Bradley opened the flood gates. He spoke of Owen's service in Afghanistan, his wife leaving him, and how they were attacked in their room in D.C. He thanked Chloe for warning them, crediting her for saving their lives. He hesitated when it came to information about himself, but as they day wore on, he told her about his dad being murdered. He painfully said that he was adopted as though he was making a confession – the strained relationship he had with Arthur after his mother died was discussed in a dignified way.

Chloe was so drawn to Bradley that she already believed she was destined to be with him. Every word he said was drawing her closer. She tingled inside, her stomach fluttered, and even her skin seemed sensitive to the air and sunshine. She was so comfortable she thought she could ask him anything, and she did.

"Bradley, I'm not a virgin," she said.

"I didn't expect you were. Premarital sex isn't the taboo it used to be," he said.

"I had an affair with a guy in college. That was it," she said, curling her lips over her teeth pressing them into a straight line.

"Okay," Bradley said.

Chloe waited. She expected a similar revelation from him. She squeezed his hand as they waded through a wave dodging a clump of seaweed. "How about you, Brad?"

"I had a sexual affair too, but it wasn't meaningful."

Chloe didn't say anything, but she was waiting for more.

"When I was in boarding school, I had an affair with a girl from the all-girls school close to our campus. She was overweight and not pretty, but very nice. She had been sexually active, but she decided that I was the only boy she wanted to do it with. She taught me all about sex." Bradley waited for a comment that never came. There was a certain intrigue in Chloe's eyes.

"She was fat, and I was fat. She wasn't embarrassed to be with me, but we were never serious. It was just a learning experience."

"You've got a body like a physical fitness trainer," Chloe said in disbelief.

"I didn't then. I still feel like a fat person inside," he said. Chloe put her arm around his waist and squeezed really hard. "I'm never going to be fat again," he added.

The beach ended at the causeway laden with gigantic rocks. They had walked more than three miles. They turned to head back the other way, Chloe still probing for information. "Why do you think those guys were trying to kill you?" she asked, moving seamlessly from Bradley's sex life onto the next subject.

"Owen thinks it was mistaken identity."

"They knew your name," Chloe said.

"They probably didn't know anything about us. Owen's theory is that someone was selling drugs out of our apartment before we got there. We don't know how long the previous occupants were gone. They just checked with the neighbors, or our mailbox – anything is possible. I just know we haven't done anything to be murdered for," Bradley said.

"I heard Owen really beat those guys up."

"I don't know where it comes from, but something happens to him – he's like a fighting machine that clicks on at just the right moment. It's like he's someone else."

"Lucky for you, I guess," Chloe said.

After that they were quiet, walking on the sand, wading in the waves as the sea came in on the sway. Bradley stayed the night.

All along West Beach Boulevard utility workers were stringing Christmas lights, steam rising from vehicles making their way along the coastline. Temperatures had dropped overnight and now people who had been wearing swimming suits and t-shirts were dressed in jackets and sweats. Robert Swag was sitting on the Cadillac fender staring into his coffee cup. His thoughts were swirling around his current situation. Back in the old days when you needed to take someone out you just went in after dark, put a bullet in them or slit their throats and you were done. It was different now. There were so many ways to get messed up. You can't sling a cat without hitting a closed circuit tv camera, and even little kids are videoing crimes in progress with cell phones. The Feds track cell phone calls, computer searches, and credit card purchases. Sal was continually suggesting that he was paranoid – too careful, but Swag knew there was no such thing as too careful.

Mario came out of the house with a coffee mug in his hand. "Where's Sal?" he asked. Swag sipped his coffee. "Sal went back to Jersey, Mario."

"Why, Bobby?"

"Sal wasn't on board, Mario. Sal wanted to do things his way."

"I wanna do things my way too, Bobby. But you haven't sent me home."

"Mario, when I say things to you, I say 'em 'cause I want you on the same page with me. You say things to me 'cause you're stupid, but I don't go around sayin' "Mario, I think you're stupid all the time". Even if you are stupid you do what I say. Sal woudn't like that. He wanted to make phone calls and take pictures of Google, and stuff like that. You wanna see the beach and drink beer at The Pink Pony. Stuff like that ain't gonna hurt nothin', but taken pictures on Google and put'n on you cell phone will get ya caught, and maybe even killed.

"Bobby, Sal was in a hurry to get this job done. It's taking a long time. Longer than I thought. Maybe longer than Mr. Triano thought." Mario said.

"Mario, I been with Carlos before he was boss. I helped make him boss, He gets pissed about some things, but I ain't scared of him. If he put out a hit on me, I'd expect someone to do the job. Even if it was you I wouldn't have no hard feelings. Carlos is like me. He's all about family. The thing about these guys and them papers. They ain't really that important, but it's all about me. I embarrassed the family. All the families in New York and Jersey and maybe over in Cleveland where the Goddamned Irish are tryin' to take over, they're laughin' at our family. I ain't gonna let that stand, Mario."

"Bobby, I heard about that, but it wasn't a big deal. Arthur Sweeney should have been rubbed out. And the thing about the papers, that was a little funny, but it wasn't a big deal."

"It was to me, Mario."

Mario went back inside the house. He met Frank in the hallway. "What ya been doing, Mario?'

"Talking to Bobby."

"What about?"

"The same thing we always talk about, but you gotta talk about something."

Palm trees, magnolias, and crepe myrtles surrounded the granite headstone in front of the Baldwin County Courthouse in Bay Minette. The Sheriff's Office occupied the rear portion of the lower level down a narrow hallway. At the end a glass window with an embedded speaker separated Lee and Tyrese from a uniformed deputy behind it. Lee flipped his badge and said, "Special Agent Ford and Jefferson.

"What can I do for you gentlemen?"

"I guess we need to see a detective."

"What about?" The deputy asked, leaning back in his chair.

"It's a long story. It's Bureau business," Lee said.

"Sheriff's here. I guess you best see him."

"That's fine," Lee said. A buzzer sounded, the clank of metal followed and a heavy door crept open. The same deputy stepped away from his window to escort them down a hallway. He stopped and turned around. "You can stay right here, I'll let the Sheriff know you want to see him." A plumber's crack was evident as his shirttail had risen above his thick gun belt as he waddled away. He stepped inside an office door and said, "Sheriff, the Feds are here about something."

"Oh, my God, what about now?"

"Didn't say."

"Well, show 'em in."

Lee walked past the deputy into the Sheriff's office. "Morning Sheriff, Special Agent Ford, and this is Special Agent Jefferson."

"Sheriff Walker Dunn," he said, suspiciously eyeing them. "Pleased," Lee said extending his hand. Dunn shook his hand lightly.

"We haven't shot anybody, or beat up anybody lately," Dunn said, sounding much like a question.

"It's nothing like that. We're working on a case and we've stumbled onto something you should know about."

"Go ahead then, I'm glad it ain't about one of my guys. You scared me a little bit. You can't even stop a drunk driver these days without people crying racism or some bullshit like that," Dunn said smiling broadly. Tyrese snorted.

Lee explained that he and Tyrese were assigned to investigate an Illegal Possession of Cultural Artifacts. Dunn was puzzled. He didn't see how anything you had in your possession that you didn't steal could be illegal. Lee didn't try to explain it. He just said it was against the law and continued. He explained that his suspects were being stalked by dangerous criminals with the intention of doing them bodily harm. They had a video showing Swag and his crew crossing the parking lot at Shelly's Seafood Company, and disappearing into the weeds, carrying lethal weapons.

"I know Shelly. He's a good ole boy. Why don't you just go down there and ask them boys for that cultural artifact stuff they're supposed to have?" Dunn said.

Lee didn't want to tell Dunn how deep they were into this case. He didn't say that Swag had already murdered Sweeney, but the evidence was insufficient to make an arrest. Reluctantly, Lee told Dunn that Owen and Bradley had been attacked in D.C. by these same people. Sheriff Dunn was standing the entire time they were talking. After some thought he rubbed his chin and asked, "Why don't the D.C. cops get a warrant out for these guys?"

"They're working on it, but the Bureau isn't privy to local cases like this," Tyrese said. Dunn rubbed his chin again, his brow furrowed as he tried to comprehend everything Lee had said. "There ain't no law against puttin' in at a local pier and walking across the parking lot, and shotguns are like worthless relatives around here. It ain't no good to have 'em, but they ain't illegal. Your video don't show much of anything. Shelly hasn't filed a trespass report, or break in, or anything like that. There's not much I can do, but I'll have our guys give Shelly's a little extra patrol. Maybe drive through the parking lot every now and then," Dunn said.

Lee and Tyrese left not feeling confident that Sheriff Dunn would be helpful in any event. Their meeting had been disappointing, so they were left with trying to manage the situation alone. With the help from the GPS tracker, they knew where Swag was holed up. The number of people was known, and thanks to face recognition all four men were identified. The fact that Sal had rented a car was the only unknown factor. They didn't know he was gone.

Lee took the scenic route from Bay Minette traveling up the coast to turn onto Ocean Beach Road and meandered around to Marina Road. Lee commented that it was a dead end. It wasn't like Swag to be without an escape route. Tyrese listened as Lee rambled on, his stream of consciousness being verbalized as they drove along. "You know, these guys are not geniuses, but they are careful. We've been onto

Swag for years, but we've never been able to pin him down. He doesn't make stupid mistakes."

"In the movies organized crime is quiet, professional, and clean, but we learned in the classroom that it's really helter-skelter sometimes. They're not sophisticated, but they're loaded with money. Cops and politicians are in their pockets, and sometimes even on the payroll," Tyrese said.

"Swag is old school. The next generation is not unsophisticated. They've been sending their kids to Ivy League schools. They have law degrees, some of them are CPA's, highly trained techies from highly accredited schools. They're changing, but this bunch we're dealing with are leftovers, but Swag is good," Lee said.

Tyrese smiled knowingly. "What?" Lee said.

"You're old school, too, and that's not an insult," Tyrese said.

Lee thought for a moment. "I am old school and I'm proud of that. You haven't been around long enough to know this, but things in the Bureau have changed. Part of us are strictly law enforcement, but the upper echelon is political. They're more interested in promoting an agenda than they are in enforcing the law."

Just then they passed Swag's hideaway. The Caddy was sitting in the driveway. "Where's Sal?" Tyrese said. "I guess we need to find out, right," Lee responded.

Chapter Twenty-Three

The breeze coming in under the roof was cool, almost cold. Shelly's Seafood Company was rushed throughout the day, all hands were hustling to stay ahead. Two shrimp boats had come in at the same time and another carrying grouper. It was the first time Owen had been given delivery duty to local restaurants, With Shelly's permission he made a detour to visit Slingerland. Bradley's job had been packing shrimp and fish on ice, but today he was assigned to peeling and deveining. It was a simple process, but he had to be taught. Pete demonstrated by firmly holding the head, inserting a small V-shaped metal device into the vein, zipping through it in one quick motion, and then pitching the shrimp onto a wire conveyor where it was doused with distilled water as it made its way to the ice trays at the other end. After a few failed attempts, Bradley successfully deveined his first shrimp. He pitched it onto the conveyor and out of character said, "Bye, little shrimp."

Pete laughed, "Just look at what a date can do for a guy's sense of humor!"

In the evening there were two galvanized buckets full of Land Shark on ice sitting at the pathway to the pavilion. Pete picked them up and headed up the pathway with Bradley following. "Back in the days of yore the ships sailing the seven seas were stocked with barrels of rum to keep the sailors happy. If I didn't know Shelly was such a kind-hearted old soldier, I'd think he was beering us up to quash our discontent," he said. Bradley snickered; his face was glowing. Pete stopped and studied him. "You really had a good time, didn't you?" Bradley grinned. His hands curled into a ball. Pete smiled, pointed at Bradley's hand. "I forgot to tell you that deveining makes your hands sore as hell until you get used to it.

"I'm okay," Bradley said.

"Owen had finished his deliveries to arrive a few minutes later. "Did you get lost today?" Pete asked. "No, I had a GPS, but Shelly let me get off the route to go see Sling"

"How was he?"

"Good. He looks great. He has a nice haircut, and he's had some major dental work. Sling said without having a fifth of whiskey a day to deaden the pain, he was miserable. They fixed his teeth and they look great, better than he did back in the day."

Bradley went over to the shower and pulled back the curtain, turned on the water and closed the curtain behind him. "It might be too cold out here for a shower, Brad. You can use the trailer shower if you want to," Pete said.

"No problem, Pete, but thanks."

Owen had a faraway expression as he turned the Land Shark in his hand. "I know Bradley's mom got a favor from her lawyer friend, but this stuff with Sling is expensive. Do you think there's some secret organization that foots the bill for this stuff, Pete?" he asked.

"I don't know, Owen, but I'm glad they do, if that's the case. I sure don't have that kind of cash myself." Owen turned up his bottle and downed what was left in it. He looked past Pete, his mind somewhere in the past, wandering down the road to "what might have beens." Finally, he said, "Buddy, I thought you would be teaching high school, or maybe a professor in a junior college somewhere."

"I thought you'd be a cop in Leesville, Kentucky." Pete said.

Owen popped another Land Shark. Pete was first to speak again. "Owen, I told you I'm happy here. You may not believe it, but this is all I want."

"It may be all I want too. That's what scares me, Pete," Owen said. Pete smiled, "Lets fuck old together, buddy," he said. Owen tilted his bottle and they clinked them in a toast. "I read that on a birthday card," Pete said.

Lee Ford and Tyrese Jefferson had driven nearly every inch of Gulf Shores and Orange Beach, even across the causeway into Florida. They talked politics, crime family history, and since they were both lawyers, they talked about laws and how to get around them. They avoided that one little sticking point that hung over them like a rain cloud. Murder was not a federal offense. Their sole reason for being there was eighteen missing pages from John Wilkes Booth's diary.

"Oh, another stain on the old banner," Lee said. Tyrese was facing the window. The sand between the road and the ocean was as white as snow. It was a section between Gulf Shores and Orange Beach that belonged to the Alabama State Park District. It was as pristine as the day it was formed.

"Lee, you know we have to contact those guys and warn them, don't you?"

"I do, but we can't question them about that stuff they have. These guys are as clean as wind driven snow. If we ask them about that shit, they'll hand it right over to us. At that point we'll have solved our Illegal Possession of Cultural Artifacts case," Lee said.

"And then we're through," Tyrese said.

"Well, I guess we'll have to avoid the subject then," Lee acknowledged.

Bradley had showered and left to meet Chloe. The Land Shark buckets were half full. Shelly walked over from the pier and sat down at the picnic table. "Thanks for the refreshments," Pete said, holding his beer, pointing with his little finger. "I don't know what you're talking about," Shelly said. "Yeah, right," Pete said.

Just at that moment Lee and Tyrese stopped at the pathway to the pavilion. Owen cranked his neck to see who was there. "Guys in suits," he said.

"Cops," Shelly said, raising his eyebrows.

Nobody moved to get up. Lee approached the picnic table showing his identification. "Hi, gentlemen, I'm Special Agent Ford, this is Special Agent Jefferson." Shelly swung his leg over the picnic table seat and stood up. "I'm Shelly Barnett, I own this property. What can I do for you?"

"We don't want to alarm you, but there's a serious situation developing concerning Owen Black and Bradley Sweeney," Lee said.

Owen raised his eyebrows as he and Pete turned around to face Lee. "What's is it?" Owen asked abruptly, a scowl deepening on his face.

At that point Lee began narrating the story, part of it Owen already knew. Lee explained that the men who attacked him in D.C. had followed them to Bon Secour. Lee awkwardly informed them that they had already been on the property with the intent to ambush them, admitting that he and Tyrese were tailing them and witnessed them proceeding into the brush in the direction of the pavilion. Pete said. "I knew it! I told you someone had been in here. I knew it!"

Tyrese added that Sheriff Walker Dunn had been informed and agreed to add extra patrol to the area. When they finished, Shelly was quick to ask, "Why don't you arrest these guys?"

"Insufficient evidence," Lee said.

Pete frowned, "Why hasn't the D.C. police department contacted us, or Is this a federal case?"

"No, it's not federal, we're looking at them for something else. We can help in the investigation if the local sheriff's department requests our help, but since murder isn't a federal crime, we don't have jurisdiction. Still, we won't stand by and watch a crime being committed without stepping in."

"If you're available, you'll step in, right?"

"Of course, and I think this case we're working on will keep us close. We'll leave a cell phone number. You can call anytime you think something suspicious is going on." Lee handed Shelly his card. "We'll do everything we can, Shelly, but I think you should call Sheriff Dunn and make a report concerning trespassing. Get it on record."

"This is serious," Owen said.

"We wouldn't be here if it wasn't."

Bradley was with Chloe at Tacky Jack's Seafood Restaurant on Canal Drive in Orange Beach. He didn't know what had developed. There was no reason for him to be uptight, but he was. Chloe was chatty, observing that Christmas lights and decorations seemed strange without cold weather. She rambled on about cars with reindeer attached to the windows and plastic Santa Clause figures climbing palm trees on the beach. It just didn't seem right. The continual lightning in the evenings fascinated her. Even at that moment it was lighting up the ocean in the distance.

"Is this normal, all this lightning?" she asked, pointing out to sea.

"I don't know, I've only been here for about a month," Bradley said.

A slender young woman in a long white dress walked out onto the long pier. She descended the ladder to the boat slip onto an outboard cabin cruiser. The white light in the distance pulsating in the clouds materialized behind her accentuating the dress and her lissome figure. Her long strides caused the slit in her dress to open exposing a shapely leg as she stepped into the boat. She fired up the engine and headed out into the bay. She was standing straight and tall, steering a route past Gilcrest Island. Her wake in the dark water was defined by white tops on the waves fulminating as she disappeared into the darkness. Bradley and Chloe watched, admiring her skill, her beauty and most of all her independence.

A look of forbearance was showing on Chloe's face. "Bradley, there's things about me you should know. You never ask anything about me, or about my past. I don't think you even know my last name," she said softly.

"I don't ask a lot of questions. I listen to people when they talk about what they like, and I watch what they do. I try not to be judgmental, but I know almost everything I want to know about people without asking questions. I don't know your last name. You're Chloe. I like everything about you. You're considerate, brave, and you're smart. I like your face and your shape, the way you walk and the sound of your voice. I don't know your last name; you're Chloe. That's all I need to know," he said.

Chloe's breath was taken away. She was anxious for the words Bradley had spoken. The moment he walked into Warburton's Bar and Grill, she wanted to hear him say something just like he had said. She was quiet, watching his face, relieved, and comforted. "Bradley, I feel everything for you that you just said about me, but I need to tell you this." She paused and took a deep breath. "I'm a hundred thousand dollars is debt. My student loan adviser is calling me every week wanting to know when I'm going to make a payment. I don't make enough money at work to catch up. I pay what I can but it's never enough."

Bradley was silent, calm, showing little emotion. Chloe continued. "My name is Chloe Bernardi. I'm from Elmira, New York. It's a rundown dinky little coal mining town. My dad is a mine supervisor, and mom works at the library. They're hard-working people, but they can't afford to help, and I wouldn't ask them to. It's my problem, but I thought you should know." Her face was strained as she was fighting back tears.

Bradley moved closer to her. He put his arm around her shoulder and squeezed. "Chloe, it's not a problem. My house in Charlottesville is worth three times more than that. My dad was murdered, and I'm the only child. He had a life insurance policy, but he probably cashed that in to get money for gambling but it doesn't matter. Either way, we're all good."

"But it's not your problem, Bradley." Chloe continued.

"It's not a problem at all. But there's two things I have to tell you, too. Things I've been keeping to myself, but I can't tell you one of them, because I have to tell Owen first. It's something that might change our relationship, but he should know. So, I've got my problems, too."

Chloe, still feeling relieved, her curiosity was now piqued. "What is it? You said you weren't gay. Are you bi-sexual?"

Bradley laughed, "No!"

"What is it?"

At that point Bradley narrated the story about finding the satchel enclosed within the walls on their work site. He explained how there were conspiracy theories for a hundred and fifty years about Edwin Stanton being involved in Abraham Lincoln's assassination. Stanton was in possession of Booth's diary, and when it was turned over to Congress there were eighteen missing pages. The building where they were working was built during that period and it was close to the Capitol. The satchel contained eighteen pages. They had only seen one of them and it said, *Another Stain on The Old Banner*. Those were the last words spoken by Booth before he was shot dead. If you let your mind run wild, it's easy enough to believe we are in possession of those eighteen missing pages.

Chloe had forgotten her own problems for the moment. She was fascinated by Bradley's narrative. "Why don't you open the satchel and read it?" she asked excitedly.

"It's complicated. There might be something in there that changes history. Maybe something negative about Lincoln. I'm satisfied with history just as it is. I know Owen thinks I'm strange, but I don't want people analyzing everything about it, changing the perspective, like they have everything else. Look at how they're trying to discredit Thomas Jefferson. The slavery issue," Bradley said.

"You have to admit slavery was awful. Jefferson owned slaves," Chloe said.

"Thomas Jefferson didn't invent slavery. He was born into it. It didn't at all seem wrong to him until he was old, a long time after the Revolution. From everything I've read about Jefferson, the man he was, he would have been a defender of civil rights in today's society. I just don't want to take a chance," Bradley said.

"Do you think there was something bad about Lincoln in Booth's diary?"

"I don't know, Chloe, but I'm not going to be the person who changes history."

Chloe didn't have to think about it long. Bradley's phone pinged. It was a message from Shelly. "Get back to Pete's as soon as you can get here."

The traffic along Ocean Boulevard was atrocious. Chloe was driving, and Bradley was in the passenger seat, staring straight ahead. It was stop and go as college boys hung out the car windows shouting at the girls walking down the sidewalk. Old people were stopped in traffic trying to make left turns into their condos without daring to turn with less than five hundred feet clearance from oncoming traffic. Bradley was patient, but his frown was growing deeper as each traffic snarl got longer. To make things worse, there was fog beginning to settle in.

"It's probably about those guys," he said.

Chloe bit her fingernail. "I was thinking that, too, Bradley. It's scary."

"Why would anyone want to harm Owen and me?" Bradley asked, more to himself than to Chloe.

"Maybe it's got something to do with that diary. Something like that would be very valuable if it was authentic," Chloe said.

"That's crazy. Nobody would think we have Booth's diary," Bradley said.

"You do." Chloe said. Bradley looked straight ahead.

After forty-five minutes they arrived at Pete's. Owen was sitting in the hammock, his legs spread with his hands dangling between his knees. Pete was leaning against the picnic table while Shelly was pacing like an agitated old lion.

Chloe followed Bradley down the pathway astonished by the premises. Her only thought was that it looked like a combination of a sawmill shed and Tarzan's house from the movies. She held Bradley's hand and tried to take it all in.

"What's up?" Bradley asked as they entered the pavilion. "Better sit down," Owen said.

"This is Chloe," Bradley turned his hand out towards Pete and Shelly, introducing them. Chloe spoke, she was pleased to meet them. She said "Hi" to Owen.

"We've got a problem," Owen said.

"What is it?"

"It turns out the guys we saw at the tiki bar were the same as the people who tried to kill us in D.C."

Chloe gasped.

"I'd ask you to go somewhere and lie low, but I want you close while we decide what to do." Owen said.

"I'm not going anywhere, Owen," Bradley said.

"Why don't you call the police?" Chloe asked.

It was a logical question. "We've talked to the FBI, but we're screwed as far as they're concerned," Pete said.

"They talked to the Sheriff, but they got the same answer from him. We're screwed," Owen said, repeating Pete's sentiments.

"In Nam we had a little trick we used that made it a little easier to sleep. We learned it from Charley – well, somebody learned it from Charley. We strung bamboo chimes all around us in the jungle. When something hit the strings, they rattled like hell. In the jungle, that shit would wake the dead. Since we don't have an alarm system around here, we could string some bamboo," Shelly said. Owen smiled. Pete walked around the picnic table to face Owen. "What would we do in Afghanistan?" Pete asked, raising his eyebrows.

"If we knew Terry was lurking, we'd find them and hit them first." Owen said.

"Who's Terry?" Chloe asked.

"Taliban," Pete said.

"I say we do that here. We find them and hit them first," Pete said.

Shelly was still pacing, but he had picked up speed. His lips were drawn tight across his teeth. "Everybody knows these bastards are here to ambush you. The Feds know about it, Dunn knows about it, and now we know it, but nobody wants to do anything. I say Pete's right. Let's find them and hit them first!"

Chloe was wide-eyed, squeezing Bradley's hand. His face was like stone, eyebrows drawn creating a deep wrinkle across his forehead. He watched Owen for a reaction. Owen stood up and began pacing, rubbing his chin. "I've killed people and broken things, and I've never been completely healed. I'm not for this, but I'm not running. I'm not hiding either, so I need to think."

"You could end up in jail," Chloe said softly.

"I'd rather be tried by twelve than carried by six," Shelly said angrily.

"We don't know where they are," Bradley said. Everybody stopped and stared at him as though the thought had never occurred to any of them, and it hadn't. They were brainstorming, but that one little detail had not been considered.

"If we find them, can we do this without killing them?" Owen asked. It was instantly quiet. Shelly stopped pacing, shoved his hands into his pockets and waited. Pete cleared his throat. "This is all arbitrary if we can't find them, but Owen, we've taken a lot of prisoners in our time. We've cleared entire houses with just a handful of guys and never fired a shot."

"Most of the time we did it under the cover of darkness. We had night vision goggles, and night optical from the air. We don't have any of that." Owen said.

Pete walked to a gray heavy-duty tarp covering an object the height of about eight feet. He jerked the tarp off like a magician clearing a tablecloth without disturbing the dishes. Beneath the tarp stood a steel cabinet, a logo stating The Bank of Milwaukee. Pete manipulated the combination lock, stopping occasionally to think. When the door opened, a stash of military gear was exposed. There was a plastic bag full of night vision goggles, a thermal vision nightscope, bulletproof vests, and several .45 caliber Colt handguns.

Shelly straightened with a jolt. "So that's where that old safe went!" he spouted. "That's all you're seeing?" Owen said.

"Oh, I knew Pete had all that stuff. I just didn't know where he was keeping it. I haven't seen that old safe in years." Shelly disappeared shortly after that. When he returned, he was carrying a fistful of heavy duty ziplock tabs. "These things are just as good as plastic handcuffs. If we're gonna take prisoners, we'll need these," he said.

Owen examined the stash, a worried expression growing on his face. "Pete, there's twenty thousand dollars-worth of equipment here. Where'd you get it?"

Pete frowned. "Sam stayed here for about a week. After he left, I found this stuff in an old car he left behind. Shelly and I looked at it. We thought it was best to lay low – stay out of it. Possession of this stuff might land me in jail, or land Sam in jail. I guess we don't have to worry about Sam now," he said.

"I guess that's the least of our worries," Owen said.

At that point they put their heads together, making plans. Special Agent Ford had left information on Swag's vehicle, the year, color and license number, just in case they might see it prowling around. It was possible that Swag and his crew were staying close to Pleasure Island Tiki Bar, since that was where they had seen them. Marina Ave was close, and there were numerous snowbird homes on that stretch, so it was a logical place to start looking. Shelly retrieved four two-way radios from the plant for communication since Pete and Owen didn't have cell phones. They were fully charged and had a range of about five miles.

Bradley and Chloe were in Chloe's car, Owen and Pete took the F150, and Shelly drove his station wagon. They went to Orange Beach and began the search. It was an outrageous plan, but all of them but Bradley were outrageous men who had lived outrageous lives.

Chapter Twenty-Four

Fog and frequent lightning flashes presented a hazard for Swag and his gang as they drove west on Water Way Boulevard. It was as thick as pea soup over Oyster Bay. The road in front of them was dark and murky in the trees along both sides of the road. Twice Swag missed the turn into the lane at Stanley's Marina. When they drove into the parking lot, the pier and dock were nearly invisible and the water in the bay was indistinguishable from the horizon. It was so dark there wasn't a single light visible anywhere.

Swag stopped the Caddy and stared straight ahead. Mario squirmed in the front seat nervously, hoping Swag would cancel their endeavor. Frank was noncommittal as usual. "I don't think we can do this without Sal. He cudda got us through this shit, but I don't think I can," Swag said.

"I'm glad to hear you say that, Bobby, I was getting a little nervous there," Mario said.

"You're always nervous, Mario. You get nervous when it lightnings. You get nervous 'cause there might be a hurricane. You're nervous 'cause a snake might bite you inna weeds. Now you're nervous 'cause there's fog."

"There's lightning, too, Bobby," Mario said.

"I know that, Mario, and for once you're right. It's too dangerous to go out into that shit tonight. I'm gonna go back to the house, but I'm stoppin' for a couple bottles a wine. I'm gonna drink enough to forget about you for a little while. Is that okay, Mario?"

"Sounds good to me, Bobby."

Little Lagoon and Cotton Bayou had disappeared into the gray mist. All along Beach Road a white curtain hung over the streets like a cloud. Waves were beating against the shore roaring in the night like a train engine, but that was the only evidence of an ocean out there. You couldn't see it from a hundred feet away.

Bradley and Chloe were on Martinique Drive, Pete and Owen were negotiating a hazardous stretch on Cove Drive, and Shelly was on Marina Road. Occasionally they talked on the two-way radios, giving updates on how much of the area they had covered. It was 10:45 p.m., and they were all thinking the same thing. Mother Nature was putting the skids on their plans. Chloe was sitting as close to Bradley as she could get, her eyes glued to the road. The live oaks with Spanish moss hanging from limbs materialized in the mist, looking like ragged arms reaching out of the fog to snatch passing cars, to devour them like a hungry gnarled monster.

"This is spooky," she said.

Bradley was driving, lurking over the stirring wheel, hoping to find Swag's car, and using caution just to keep the car between the lines.

"This is like a Frankenstein movie. I wouldn't be surprised to see the villagers coming out of the trees with torches and pitchforks," Chloe said.

Bradley didn't have the chance to answer. Shelly was on Marina Road, making a U-turn from Tacky Jacks. "Breaker, I got an eyeball on this car. It passed me heading east on Marina Road," Shelly said excitedly.

"That's a dead end, isn't it?" Pete asked.

"You got that right," Shelly said.

 "Don't lose it."

"I'm on it like white on rice," Shelly said.

Bradley had to use the GPS, but Pete knew the area well. He and Owen were on Marina Road quickly. Owen suggested they meet in Tacky Jacks parking lot and wait for Shelly to come back with an address. It didn't take long. "Breaker, breaker, 2723 Marina Road," Shelly shouted into the portable radio.

"We got it, Shelly. Meet us at Tacky Jacks."

Now they knew the address. They decided to hit Swag before he hit them. They knew they were vulnerable, defenseless, and without any support from law enforcement. The FBI told them they were being stalked and confirmed they were in danger. Waiting for Swag to come after them wasn't an option, but going after Swag didn't feel right either. Owen wasn't afraid of Swag. He was reluctant to go through with it because he thought things might get out of hand and he would kill them all. They were all together in the parking lot, Owen was pacing. Pete knew what he was thinking.

"Owen, we have to do this, or you and Bradley have to run." Pete said

"I'm not afraid of these guys, Pete. I'm afraid of what I'll do. I may lose it and kill every one of them."

"That wouldn't be anything they don't deserve," Pete said.

"It's taken me a long time to get back to normal – if I ever was normal, but I don't want to live the rest of my life waking up in the middle of night with masses of dead bodies meandering around in my head," Owen said.

"Owen, I'm confident we were on the right side of things in Afghanistan, but it still keeps me up sometimes," Pete said.

"We were on the right side of things, and we're on the right side now, but it makes me wonder if I'm always going to be fighting for my life." He hesitated for a long pause. "I'm not afraid of these bastards, but they should be afraid of me."

Owen was adamant about leaving Bradley out, but Bradley was just as adamant about staying in. They were at loggerheads, but Bradley finally won out. As it stood, they would wait until the lights went out at 2723 Marina Dr., and then they would make a move. They had all the equipment they needed to make a clean sweep, take all prisoners, and come out without anyone dying. Shelly's old wagon would be their transportation, because it was a rusty brown color and would meld into the night. When they left Chloe at

Pleasure Island Tiki Bar, she kissed Bradley and said, "I love you."

Noise from The Pink Pony was filtering through the fog where Lee was soaking up ambiance from the balcony. The colored lights, music, and people milling around on the deck softened by fog, elevated the little pink bar in stature. It almost looked inviting.

Tyrese walked out onto the balcony. "I got a text from the tech lab. They're sending an e-mail with an update." They went back inside and placed the computer on the coffee table. When Tyrese opened the lid, the e-mail was already there. He clicked onto it and started reading. When they finished, both men were astounded. Part of it was shocking, but both were suddenly jacked up. And ready. Lee was pacing, trying to absorb what they had just seen and read. Tyrese had his hands in his pockets, waiting for Lee to make a decision. "We need an arrest warrant, but every minute we waste is like a ticking time bomb for Black and Sweeney," Lee said. "We could contact the Bureau and maybe get a judge out of bed," Tyrese said.

"You ever known a federal judge to get out of bed this time of night to issue a warrant?"

Tyrese exhaled, "No, I was just thinking out loud," he said.

"When I was a Pittsburg Police Detective, we made arrest all the time without a warrant. We've got probable cause to go after Swag, especially now that we have some real direct evidence," Lee said, pointing to the computer. "It's the

Bureau, they don't want bad press. Take the safe way all the time. It's all political these days."

"Let's do it," Tyrese said.

"Call Sheriff Dunn, tell him we're going in. "

Marina Road was gloomy. Shelly had negotiated the station wagon across the ditch and parked as deep into the trees as he could get it. The tv set was flashing dimly; the only light visible in Swag's house. Everything else was black. Owen was in the driver's seat, Pete on the passenger side, and the other two were in the back. "That tv light is probably coming from the living room," Shelly said, leaning forward. Nobody said anything.

Pete opened the door and the dome light came on. Shelly lunged for it, pushing the switch to the off position. "That sonofabitch hasn't been on in ten years, and now it works!" he snorted.

"It's not a big deal, Shelly. They couldn't see us if they were standing ten feet away," Owen said, smiling at his reaction.

"I thought we might all take a look through these night vision goggles – get habituated to them," Pete said. Everybody thought it was a good idea, each of them giving it a try. "My God, it's like daylight, even in the fog'" Shelly exclaimed. Owen declined because he already knew everything about them. Pete was leaning over the car fender, the thermal imaging night goggles over his eyes. "There's two subjects in the living room, one of them is moving." Both were merely glowing light, created by body heat, vaguely outlined – just well enough to recognize them as human bodies.

A light came on shortly thereafter, confined to a small area away from the tv light. "One of them is taking a piss, I guess," Pete said. At that point the other glowing orb approached the front door, a man stepped outside. He walked away from the door, unzipped and urinated in the yard. "I guess they both had to go at the same time," Shelly said.

"That's only two. Shouldn't there be another guy?" Owen asked.

"He could be in a deeper part of the house, I'll wait 'til they go to bed before I get closer. We need to get up close to disable the electricity anyway," he said. Bradley took his turn viewing the area with the night vision goggles. He was as amazed as Shelly had been, but he didn't comment. He got back into the car. Owen was still in the driver's seat. "I'm a little nervous, Owen." he said.

"I'm a little nervous too, buddy, but everything will be alright."

The house went completely dark. Pete and Shelly got back into the car. "I've got an idea how the house is laid out by the movement on the thermal goggles. This door closest to us is to the kitchen, there's a hallway from the living room to two bedrooms. By the way the orbs are situated, two of these guys are in bed. The tv light is turned off now, and I've got a weak signal from the other side of the house. I think that's the master bedroom," Pete said.

"We'll have to disable the electricity," Shelly said. He held up a battery-powered screwdriver. "In these older ranch houses the electrical box to the main electrical service entrance is on the outside. There are four screws holding the cover on. We just need to take the cover off and throw the switch," he said. "This thing is quiet," he added, waving the screwdriver. "That kitchen doorknob can be disassembled in twenty seconds and we'll be in like Flynn."

Owen walked around to Pete's side of the car and squatted on his haunches. The others gathered around him. "Everybody will line up behind me once that doorknob is off. I want Pete behind me, Bradley behind Pete, and Shelly comes in last. I'm heading for that back bedroom. Pete and Bradley, you take the second bedroom down the hallway. Shelly, give them time to go in, and then you take your guy. Have we got those heavy duty ziplock tabs?"

Shelly pulled a handful of plastic strips from his pocket and gave everybody several of them. "Pete and I have .45s. If we have to use them, you don't have to worry about leaving anyone standing. This right here will take down a bull with one shot," Owen said. He stood up and examined the ziplocks. "Everybody, familiarize yourself with these." He threaded the end of the plastic through the opening and cinched it shut. He pulled hard trying to open it and it held tight. The other three followed suit.

Owen reached into the back seat and pulled out two double-barrel shotguns. He handed one of them to Bradley. "This is a deadly sonofabitch. There is nothing better at close range. All you have to do is point and pull the trigger. It has a hammer on both chambers. You just pull the hammer back and squeeze and, bam! It's all over for anybody in the way." He broke it down and shoved two 12-gauge buckshot shells into the chamber. "Remember Brad, pull the hammer back on both chambers and squeeze," he said. His lips tightened and the muscles in his jaw were drawn tight. "I hope we don't have to use it."

"Keep it in mind, with these goggles we can see them, but they can't see us," Pete said.

Shelly took the other shotgun, nodded affirmatively at Owen. His kindly old eyes full of compassion. "These sonofabitches came for us, Owen. We didn't go looking for this kind of madness."

Owen nodded back.

"Let's roll," Owen said.

Lee and Tyrese were on Ocean Boulevard inching along behind two lanes of traffic, Tyrese was on his cell phone updating Sheriff Dunn on the situation. Several times Dunn asked Tyrese if he was sure they had the goods on Swag. Tyrese assured him in every way possible, but he sensed Dunn was still doubtful. Finally, Dunn agreed to assist, and he would bring three units to back them up.

Owen and Shelly walked along the roadside until they reached the far side of the house. Two cars passed them with hazard lights flashing. Shelly peeled off, stiff legged, bent at the waist. He hurried across the yard to the electrical box. As promised, the lid was removed quickly, the switch thrown, and all electrical was disabled. Pete and Bradley were waiting at the kitchen door. Shelly worked his magic again on the lock. In short order, the door was open. Owen leaned over at the waist, bent his knees and prepared to move forward. Pete stretched both arms across Owen's shoulder, pointing the .45 caliber automatic straight into the dark room. Bradley followed Pete's lead and then Shelly. Owen advanced through the kitchen, Pete, Bradley and Shelly moved in single file down the hallway. Pete and Bradley advanced past the first bedroom. Shelly stopped, squatted on his haunches, and waited. Pete led the way into the bedroom. Frank was lying in bed. He was awake looking at the ceiling. Some small noise caused him to look at Pete moving towards him.

"Mario, is that you?"

Pete shoved the .45 against his head. "Don't move, motherfucker, or make a sound." Pete growled.

Frank gasped. Bradley straddled him on the bed, stuck the double barrel shotgun against his throat. "Close your mouth," he said. Pete grabbed a roll of duct tape from his fatigue pocket, slapped it over Frank's mouth and rolled it all the way around his head. "Turn over, you sonofabitch!" he whispered. Frank rolled over and put his face into the pillow. Bradley stuck the shotgun into Frank's groin, steadied it with his knee and zip tied his wrists together. "You're a quick learner," Pete whispered.

Pete signed for Bradley to stay with Frank. Bradley pulled Frank onto the floor, placed him face down, and rested the shotgun barrel against the back of his neck. Frank was as still as a petrified log.

Mario was aroused by the quiet rustling, tried to turn on the lamp but found it inoperable. He shook it, and then cursed. He got out of bed and walked into the hallway. Shelly rammed his shotgun into Mario's belly. "What the fuck!" he exclaimed. Pete closed in on him, shoved the .45 into his face and said, "Open you're fucking mouth."

Mario's eyes were like saucers as he stared into a face covered by night vision goggles. He had never seen anything like it. It was bizarre and frightening. Pete might as well have been an invader from outer space, but Mario recognized the .45 and knew what it could do so his mouth dropped open in a flash. Pete stuck the barrel into Mario's throat. "Don't make a sound. Put your hands behind you."

Mario complied. Shelly cuffed him, kicked the back of his knee and Mario went down with a thud. With the skill he had developed zip locking plastic bags full of shrimp, Shelly, in one fluid motion, strapped Mario's legs together as quick as a cowboy hobbling a runaway calf in a rodeo. Pete looked on in admiration. Shelly's heart was thumping in his chest. "I hope I don't have a fucking heart attack before we get these motherfuckers put where they belong," he said, breaking for a deep breath.

Owen slipped quietly into Swag's room. He was sitting in a stuffed chair beside the bed, an empty wine bottle on the floor, and another half empty on the lamp table lying on its side with a stream of red liquid trailing off onto the floor. Swag was snoring. A .38 revolver was showing beneath the pillow on the bed. "Wake up," Owen said in a normal tone. Swag opened his eyes. "Turn on the fuckin' light, Mario."

"It's not Mario. It's Owen Black."

Swag's eyes widened. Lights from a passing car brightened the room. "What the fuck do you want?" Swag demanded.

"You're under arrest," Owen said.

"You ain't no fuckin' cop!"

"Citizen's arrest," Owen said.

Swag snorted, "Citizens arrest for what, asshole!"

"Stalking, with the intent to kill somebody,"

"Ha! There ain't no such fuckin' charge!" Swag said.

"This .45 I have pointing at your head says there is. Get on your knees." Another car light cut the darkness, and then faded.

"You're fuckin' hand's shaking. You're scared," Swag said.

"I can shoot with my left hand," Owen said.

"You ain't got no nerve."

"My handshakes because I'm trying to restrain myself. It does that when I'm about to do some real damage. Right now, I've got this .45 in my hand and I don't have much restraint left. Now get on your knees."

"I ain't gett'n on my knees for nobody. If you're gonna shoot me, you gotta do it with me standin' up." Swag pushed against the chair arms and became erect. "I'm getting' that

.38 right there, and one of us is goin' to the boneyard." he snarled.

Owen's right hand was shaking, his brow furrowed, lips drawn tight. In one swift movement Owen hurled the .45 at Swag's head. It hit the mark, splitting his scalp open. Instantly blood was flowing. Owen went into a crouch, sprang forward and slammed his elbow across Swag's jaw, simultaneously throwing his knee into his groin. Swag bent forward, Owen pushed his head down and tomahawked his back, a blow that was often deadly. Swag went forward onto his face and lie gasping for breath. Owen ratcheted his arms behind him, and zip locked them together. "Like I said, You're under arrest for something or another."

Shelly's Seafood Company squad dragged their prisoners into the front yard and placed them face down, all in a row. Shelly called 911. The radio dispatcher said the sheriff was already on his way.

Bradley grabbed four chairs from the kitchen, and they all sat in a circle around their prisoners.

"I suppose we'll all be arrested," Pete said.

"Like Shelly said, better be tried by twelve than be carried by six," Owen said.

"I don't know what things are like in Kentucky, Owen, but there ain't no jury in Alabama going to convict us on something that's clearly self-defense. We'll call the FBI agents that warned us as witnesses. We can identify these dudes from the tiki bar. You and Bradley had to beat their asses in D.C., and that bartender can tell his story. We're in like Flynn, I tell ya."

Owen looked at Bradley. "What do you think, Brad?"

Bradley shrugged. "I think we cuss a lot when we're making an arrest," he said.

They all laughed. The relief was evident in their faces. Their expressions were reminiscent of Paul Newman, George Kennedy, and the prison work crew in Cool Hand Luke after they had tarred the prison road in a rebellious expose in courage and determination.

Lee and Tyrese were driving slowly down Marina Road. Four Baldwin County squad cars with lights flashing red and blue color into the fog was like a neon cloud streaming down the street. When they reached 2723 Marina Rd, Lee saw four vague figures in the yard materializing through the haze. He shined his spotlight exposing them, and then he saw Swag and his gang lying face down in the grass.

"What's all this?" he said, his jaw dropping in amazement.

"It's Black and Sweeney and those other two guys," Tyrese said.

Sheriff Dunn was first to exit his car, followed by three uniformed deputies. They stormed the group shouting and gnarling like a pack of wild dogs. "Get your hands up. Get down on the ground!"

Shelly stood up with his hands above his head. "They got us, boys," he said cheerfully. A deputy ran at Shelly sticking his nine-millimeter into his face. "Get down on the ground!" he shouted.

"I'm old and I'm stiff from doing your job, I need a minute, son," Shelly said as he grunted placing his knees on the ground. Owen, Pete and Bradley all settled face first into the grass. Another deputy hurried to wrap their wrist behind them with plastic handcuffs. As they lie on the ground, there was no telling the good guys from the criminals.

Swag was still hurting from the second beating he had garnered in his life from Owen Black. A gap in his head was trailing blood down his face, his lungs were struggling to recover from the tomahawk blow Owen had administered to disable him.

"Get these guys up," Lee ordered.

"We need to know what's going on here first," Sheriff Dunn said angrily.

"We know them, they're not dangerous," Tyrese said. Sheriff Dunn snorted.

Pete turned his head sideways in the grass. "They were gonna fucking kill us! We just hit them first," he shouted.

"I know what you're saying, boy, but there ain't no vigilante justice happening in my county. You're all under arrest."

Lee approached Swag, rolled him over, and said, "Robert Swag, you're under arrest for murder, intrastate gambling, and conspiracy to commit murder. And one other thing, you're under arrest for conspiracy to illegally possess cultural artifacts."

Tyrese chuckled.

"What the fuck," Swag moaned.

Mario raised his head as high as he could get it and shouted, "You don't know who you're messing with, that's Bobby Swag!" A fat deputy charged Mario and gave him a swift kick in the ribs. "Shut up, you sombitch!" he gnarled.

Tyrese shouted for the deputy to stand down, taking a position between them. The deputy was breathing hard, his face full of unexplained anger. He stepped back mumbling ethnic vulgarities. Tyrese went about assisting Owen and the others off the ground.

Lee approached another heavy-set deputy and said, "Give me your pocketknife, and don't tell me you don't have one." Begrudgingly, he fetched a knife from his pocket and handed it to Lee. "These are my prisoners," Sheriff Dunn said as Lee went about cutting loose the plastic handcuffs from Shelly and then the others. "I don't want to argue about jurisdiction, but one of your deputies just battered a defenseless man in your custody, so maybe we can negotiate."

"The last time I heard, battery wasn't a federal offense, so that'd be my concern," Dunn said.

"No, but violation of civil rights is," Lee said, looking straight into Sheriff Dunn's blank face.

Dunn turned around and shouted, "Help get these handcuffs off these guys, and put them Goddamn Yankees into the squad cars and take 'em in!"

From that point it was easy sailing. Lee followed Shelly back to Pleasure Island Tiki Bar where Chloe was waiting. When she saw Bradley, she ran and threw her arms around him and cried happily. The bar was closing, lights were dim as the bartender and waitresses cleaned up. The FBI and the vigilantes sat on the deck while Owen explained in detail how they had captured one of New Jersey's most dangerous criminals. Lee had a pretty good package of evidence too, but John Linderman would have to be the first in line to get the details. They walked through the parking lot together, the fog still thick, a foghorn blaring an eerie sound out in the darkness putting a period on the saga. Lee put his hands in his pockets, turned to face the others. "We'll be in contact with you all if we need you, but I don't think we will."

The state crime lab was called in to secure Swag's house and recover evidence, although it was just a matter of procedure. But before they arrived, Lee made a cursory search taking with him one single item, a simple sheet of paper. Owen was getting into the F150 when Lee shouted for him to wait. Lee approached him, handed Owen a vanilla folder, and then turned and walked back to his car. Owen stepped into his truck. Pete was already in the passenger seat. Owen opened the folder and saw a sheet of aged yellow paper. *So another stain on the old banner* was written across the page.

Back in D.C., it was spitting snow, and although the leaves on the oak and maple trees were flush with brilliant color, the clouds were gray, hanging low, making it look like the darkest days of winter. Lee picked Tyrese up at his apartment and drove to the FBI office on Fourth Street. They were both well rested after making their trip from Gulf Shores back to D.C. Both were wearing satisfied expressions, both within their own thoughts, but it was all about their triumphant return. "This is sweet revenge," Lee said, without any discussion prior to his statement. It didn't matter, Tyrese knew what he was talking about.

"He sent us on a wild goose chase, but it actually put a feather in our caps," Tyrese said.

"He was screwing with me, but I get the last word, don't I?" Lee said.

"Yep, but remember, you did lose Edward Snowden. That's still a considerable hole to crawl out of," Tyrese said wryly, and then he chuckled.

"Something like that," Lee said.

When they entered Linderman's office Tyrese had his laptop tucked under his arm. He awkwardly changed it from his right arm to the left. Extending his hand to Linderman, he said, "Chief."

"Good to see you again, Trace."

"Ah, that's Tyrese, Chief."

"That's what I said, Tyrese."

Lee walked to the chair in front of Linderman's desk, casually unbuttoned his jacket and took a seat. Tyrese nervously settle into a chair beside him.

"I guess the story about Swag's arrest has broken, and it seems like the talking heads know more about his history than we do," Linderman said.

"I haven't heard anything. We've been putting our reports together since we got in, John," Lee said. Tyrese powered up his laptop and placed it in front of Linderman. He leaned over and pointed to the keyboard. "Just hit that button right there, John," he said. Linderman scowled and shot Tyrese a perturbed glance. "I mean, Chief," Tyrese said apologetically.

The computer came to life displaying a screen shot of Arthur Sweeney sitting at the keyboard. The audio recorder and computer video were rolling. The entire conversation between Swag and Sweeney was recorded. Linderman watched and listened, focused on every word, and then there was a blast - blood splattered on the screen, the picture shook radically, and then it was still. Swag's face became visible behind blood running down the screen. He reached across Sweeney's body and retrieved a sheet of paper. "Thank you, Dr. Sweeney, I'll let myself out," he sneered. Linderman reeled away from the screen, shocked by what he had seen. "God, that's gory! But really good," he laughed.

"Sweeney was a drunk, and a loser, but a pretty smart guy. He had hidden files with names, dates, and detailed accounts of his losses, and his visits from Swag," Lee said. "Swag didn't have any idea he was being videoed," Lee added.

"How far does it go?"

"All the way to Carlos Triano," Tyrese said.

"Not bad for my old ex-brother-in-law, even if you did lose Snowden," Linderman said, giving Lee a thumbs up.

Tyrese's eyes widened. He gasped, "You said Snowden!"

"Something like that," Linderman said, smiling respectfully at Lee.

When the meeting was over, in the hallway, Tyrese asked Lee if he was satisfied with Linderman's response. "Do you think he's eating crow over our success?" he asked.

"I'm a forgiving kind of guy, Tyrese. I don't really care to rub his nose in it. He seemed happy for us actually," Lee said. "How about that other thing?" Tyrese said, looking at Lee sideways. Lee didn't answer, Linderman was coming down the hallway. As they entered the elevator, he hurried to catch them."Hey, what happened to the cultural artifacts case?" he said.

As the door closed Lee said, "There wasn't anything to it, John."

Behind the closed doors Tyrese was ready to pop. "Goddammit, Lee, I want some details!" he said almost in a shout.

Lee shrugged. "His sister's a bitch and he knows it. If he could, he would say I stayed with her too long," he said.

"You know that's not what I mean! I don't care about you being divorced from the boss' sister, although maybe you should have told me. It's the other thing. Come on, give it up!"

"Oh, Edward Snowden. Yeah, I read about that in the newspaper."

Chapter Twenty-Five

Christmas morning in Bon Secour, Alabama, was sunny and the mercury was holding at 52 degrees. Pete secured two overhead natural gas heaters from the plant and purchased an eight-burner gas range with an oven and broiler. Chloe and Cindy, Pete's young lady friend, the girl who he thought would see the light and run off with someone more her age, strung Christmas lights and prepared Christmas dinner. The aroma from turkey roasting in the oven permeated the air. A tablecloth with reindeer pictures and Santa Clause covered the picnic table, and Christmas tunes on Pete's boom box accorded the pavilion a remarkable holiday ambiance.

Shelly had sweatshirts made with Shelly's Seafood Company Vigilantes printed on the chest and handed them out with great fanfare. The men brandishing their benign chauvinism sat around drinking wine and occasionally opening the oven to check on the turkey. When they sat down for dinner Shelly offered up a toast. "To all that we are, and all that we will be," he said, with everyone reaching across the table to clink glasses. "I stole that from a movie," he added.

They ate and drank and laughed until late in the afternoon. When the table was cleaned and everything put away, there was nothing left but to sit at the picnic table and groan about having eaten too much. Shelly took a spoon and pinged his glass several times. He stood up, a strained expression growing on his face. He focused on Pete, his lips tight, a combination between a smile and an attempt to fight off tears, he said, "Pete, you've been like a son to me. I love you, brother, so I thought this would be a good time to do this."

It was as quiet as a moment in church right before the minister begins to pray at a funeral. Everybody was instantly nervous. Shelly cleared his throat. "Pete, I'm retiring. I want to sit on the benches Brad made for me and gaze on creation. I want you to have Shelly's Seafood Company. It's yours. I'll take a little of the profits, but you're the new owner."

"I can't do that, Shelly," Pete said. "It wouldn't be the same without you hanging around in there from three in the morning until eight in the evening."

"Pete, don't break an old man's heart," Shelly said, his eyes beginning to turn red.

Owen reached across the table and slapped Pete on the back. "Congratulations, Pete," he said with a wide grin. Chloe and Cindy hugged Shelly, and he hugged them back. "Pete, I'll be right out there on the pier. I'm not going anywhere, but the business is yours. It's already done."

"Thank you, you old bony warrior," Pete said.

With that said, Shelly wandered off towards the pier. Cindy settled against Pete, and Chloe and Bradley puttered around taking down Christmas lights. Owen walked out across the parking lot. He was happy for Pete, but he didn't really see himself working for Shelly's for the rest of his life. The water was like glass, cool and blue with the sunlight casting a swath of gold across the bay into the Gulf of Mexico.

"Now what do I do?" he said to himself out loud.

Bradley's voice came from behind him, "Now what do we do, Owen?" he said.

"Brad."

"Now what do we do, Owen?"

"I don't know, Brad. I wish I knew," Owen said, peering out across the bay.

"I thought maybe we could go to Alaska, build that lodge, and run the search and rescue operation. You could teach me everything you know about survival and rescue. We could do something that really matters." Bradley said. "Of course, Chloe would come too." he added

"That would take money, Brad."

"I've got money, Owen."

"No, I mean it would take a lot of money, real money" Owen said, a slight smile forming across his lips. This is a great kid, he thought.

"I've got a lot of money, Owen."

Owen looked at Bradley curiously.

"My mother's maiden name was Margret Ann Tuerbrecht." he said.

Owen stared at Bradley in disbelief. "Ahh, you mean the reclusive billionaire, Margret Ann Tuerbrecht?" Shock at that moment would be an understatement. A joke, maybe, but Bradley didn't joke.

Bradley nodded, whispered yes.

The daughter of shipping mogul Frank Tuerbrecht? The Tuerbrecht Corporation, Tuerbrecht Towers in Montreal, one of the richest men in the world!"

"Yes, Mom was sole heir, but I'm not a billionaire. She gave most of her fortune to charities across the world. She said money was the root of all evil. Our neighbors in Charlottesville didn't even know who she was. She didn't want me to be ruined by money, and she made me promise not to let it."

Owen was stunned. "Was it you who took care of the bill for Slingerland, the lawyer, the rehab, the Holiday Inn?"

"Yes. Are you mad?" Bradley was looking at Owen; a guilty expression across his face.

"How much money do you have?"

"Mom left Arthur a million. He gambled it all away, and he scammed me for a few million, but I still have a lot left. The house belongs to me." Bradley hesitated as though he was about to make a confession. "She left me forty-five million," he said sheepishly. Owen's face turned white. "You're shittin' me, Bradley!"

"Are you mad, Owen?"

"Not mad. Not mad at all," Owen said laughing out loud.

"Are we going to Alaska?" Bradley asked, a look of anticipation on his face.

"You bet we are, buddy!" Owen said, slapping Bradley's palm.

Robert Swag was found guilty of murder, intrastate gambling, extortion and conspiracy to commit murder. He is currently serving two life sentences without parole in Reed Onion State Prison in Wise County, Virginia. After a month he pretty much ran the place.

Frank Fortillo turned state's evidence and is currently in The Federal Witness Protection Program.

Mario Santano was convicted of conspiracy to commit murder and sentenced to fifteen years in the Alabama Department of Corrections.

Carlos Triano's organization attracted so much attention to organized crime in New York City and New Jersey, that Carlos is now sleeping with the fishees.

Sal Lomilino was convicted of conspiracy to commit murder and sentenced to seven years in the Alabama Department of Corrections.

Carl Slingerland recovered from alcoholism and depression. He works for Pete at Shelly's Seafood Company and is currently the operating manager of Shelly's Original Seafood House, and two thriving branch seafood outlets. Shelly Barnett spends his days watching over creation from what he calls Bradley's bench.

Pete Findley married Cindy. They have two boys and a girl. Pete still owns Shelly's Seafood Company and has begrudgingly gotten used to wearing a suit.

Owen, Bradley and Chloe built a wilderness lodge in Alaska. They have a search and rescue program, assisting governmental authorities in rescue operations. To-date they have rescued over a hundred people.

Bradley and Chloe have a son. His name is Owen, named after Uncle Owen Black. Arthur Sweeney has a permanent home on the mantel in the great room in the Shelly Barnett Gatehouse Lodge.

Chapter Twenty-Six

Whatever happened to the eighteen missing pages from John Wilkes Booths diary?

On April 15th, 2016, Leesville, Kentucky citizens gathered at the newly constructed elementary school ahead of the dedication and christening. A crisp wind was blowing dead leaves across the parking lot as teachers held down their skirts and ties. Banners and streamers behind them were flapping wildly in the wind ready at any moment to take flight.

Susan Black was handing out leaflets as people walked through admiring the facilities under the gaze of Abraham Lincoln. The hallway was lined with his pictures and paintings, grim and solemn, his eyes focused on admirers who were taking it all in. Lincoln was born a stone's throw from Leesville, but this was the first school in town that had been named in his honor.

A quote by the martyred President in bold blue letters beneath the pictures said, "Upon the subject of education, not presuming to dictate any plan or system representing it, I can only say I view it as the most important subject which we as a people can be engaged in." Above the gravest photograph it said, "Now he belongs to the ages."

Bradley Sweeney was a strange kid, growing up in the company of a reclusive mother who sheltered him from the world because she had lived her life under a microscope. His father was a self- destructive blowhard who humiliated him at every opportunity.

Bradley was rescued by Owen Black.

They found something together, extracted from behind a plastered wall. It might have been a history altering document, or it might have been nothing at all.

However, there was a certainty to what they had found. It was a concrete testament to Bradley Feeney's arrival into the real world, and redemption. If it came to pass that Owen insisted on opening the satchel – to expose it to the world, he wouldn't resist. It was for Owen to decide.

 Owen thought it was quirky and strange, but If Bradley wanted that satchel sealed, it would be sealed. He didn't need to know what was inside, and after all the trouble it had wrought, he didn't care. Still, he wanted it to have a fitting end. With that in mind, they devised a plan.

A new black Ford F150 stopped in the Abraham Lincoln Elementary School parking lot. Owen stepped out of the back seat, stopped for a long moment and looked at Bradley and Chloe. "We'll be right here when you get back, Owen" Bradley said. "We love you, Owen," Chloe said.

Owen didn't notice the cold wind or the cyclone of dry leaves mounting skyward. The anticipation of what was coming was growing with each step. It was like the day he was discharged, stepping back into civilian life. Susan saw him crossing the sod, his expression grim yet considerate. Her breath becoming shorter, she could feel her heart throbbing in her chest. She knew he would be there today, but that didn't make it any easier. An athletic man beside her placed his hand on her elbow and said, "It's okay." She looked at him with an uncertain emotion showing in her eyes. "It's okay," he said again.

Susan met Owen at the door. "We can go somewhere private," she said. Owen followed her to a secluded room. The smell of new paint permeated the air.

"You look good," she said.

"You haven't changed," Owen said.

They were quiet, neither knowing where to go from there. Finally, Susan said, "I'm grateful for everything you've done – the money you sent from Washington when you were struggling, and now the college funds for the girls, it's, it's……"

"Stop, Susan. It's all good. It's my responsibility. You don't have to be grateful." Owen said. Susan sighed, "Thank you."

It was still uncomfortable, but they managed to move on. Owen handed Susan a manila envelope containing the sheets of paper that had been stashed behind the seat of his old F150. She already knew what was enclosed. She agreed not to open it, but she was intrigued.

A time capsule was being placed into a tube at the base of the cornerstone of the new school. Newspapers, sports memorabilia, and handwritten predictions from the students would be going into it, and now, eighteen pages of a one hundred and fifty-year old mystery. Owen felt a sense of closure when he handed it to Susan. It was the end of a long goodbye.

 Owen returned to the truck, stopped, and looked back at Susan. He waved. She waved back. "Another stain on the old banner," he said to himself, and then stepped into the truck where Bradley and Chloe's eyes were focused on him.

"Vigilantes, let's roll," he said. They all raised their fists and cheered.

The End

9 781961 504097